SO-AKL-987

OTHER YEARLING BOOKS YOU WILL ENJOY:

WHEN THE BOYS RAN THE HOUSE, *Joan Carris*
WITCH-CAT, *Joan Carris*
DEAR MR. HENSHAW, *Beverly Cleary*
HENRY HUGGINS, *Beverly Cleary*
HENRY AND BEEZUS, *Beverly Cleary*
HENRY AND THE CLUBHOUSE, *Beverly Cleary*
HENRY AND THE PAPER ROUTE, *Beverly Cleary*
HENRY AND RIBSY, *Beverly Cleary*
SOUP FOR PRESIDENT, *Robert Newton Peck*
SOUP ON WHEELS, *Robert Newton Peck*

YEARLING BOOKS are designed especially to entertain and enlighten young people. Charles F. Reasoner, Professor Emeritus of Children's Literature and Reading, New York University, is consultant to this series.

For a complete listing of all Yearling titles, write to Dell Publishing Co., Inc., Promotion Department, 6 Regent Street, Livingston, N.J. 07039.

Pets, Vets, and Marty Howard

by

Joan Carris

illustrated by Carol Newsom

A YEARLING BOOK

Published by
Dell Publishing Co., Inc.
1 Dag Hammarskjold Plaza
New York, New York 10017

Dedication and Acknowledgments

With fondness and appreciation, this book is dedicated to Dr. Amos Stults and the staff of his veterinary hospital in Hopewell, New Jersey. All of these folk endured months of my questioning, wondering, and ignorance without laughter or obvious frustration, and I thank them: Dr. Amos Stults, Dr. Phyllis Reed, Dr. Ray Hostetter, Dr. Amos Stults, Jr. (Bud), Dr. Mark Smith, and Dr. Oliver Elbert.

Yearling ® TM 913705, Dell Publishing Co., Inc.

ISBN: 0-440-46855-8

Reprinted by arrangement with J. B. Lippincott, a division of Harper & Row, Publishers, Inc.

Printed in the United States of America

March 1987

10 9 8 7 6 5 4 3 2 1

CW

Contents

1.
Marty's Announcement

Marty waited until after supper to make his announcement. He didn't want anyone distracted by how many cherries there were in the Jell-O. He didn't want everyone praising Nick for another 100 on a spelling paper. He especially didn't want Jut reminding the family about his important basketball game on Friday night.

What Marty wanted was everyone paying attention to him. So he waited until they were in the living room. His parents were reading the paper, Jut was studying sophomore world history, and Nick was drawing a picture of Eleanore and her kittens. Gus had been put to bed, but since he was only four he wouldn't be interested

anyway. The family's old basset, Pierpont, snored by Mr. Howard's feet.

Marty cleared his throat. "I got the job," he said at last. "I start tomorrow after school."

Jut looked up. "Hey, that's great! I didn't think Old Doc would go for it, not a seventh grader anyway."

Mrs. Howard put down her paper. "What job, Martin?"

"Ditto for me," Marty's dad said.

"With Old Doc Cameron at the vet hospital. I said I was going to ask if she wanted help, and she does. Me."

Marty's parents looked at one another, and Mr. Howard put his paper down on the couch. "Is this a regular job with regular hours? You have a lot of homework this year. Seventh grade is enough of a job, if you ask me . . . which you didn't." He smiled at Marty.

"I agree with your father," Mrs. Howard said. "The summer you worked for Rusty Timmons's Service—taking care of all those pets—nearly finished me off. Schoolwork is enough."

"But that was different," Marty protested. "I did lots of that here at home. This time I'll be at Doc's office. Working with Old Doc will be educational, just like school. Think of what I can *learn* there."

Mr. Howard continued to smile. "Very clever, son, and I'd buy it except for one thing. How much time are you planning to give this job?"

"Just after school. I'll be here for supper and have all evening to study. Then . . . I could help Doc some on Saturdays and study on Sunday. Half school, half work. That's fair."

"When do you play?" His mother was not smiling.

Marty frowned at her. "Since when does a kid get picked on for not playing? Anyway, I can go to movies on Friday or Saturday nights with Tim and the other guys. You *know* how I like working with animals. For me, it's playing— only I'll get paid for it. How many people do you know who get paid for doing their favorite thing?"

Mr. Howard looked at Marty's mother. "Does it seem to you that we're losing this argument?" he asked her.

"Yes, only I'm not sure why. Aren't we the parents, and isn't he the child?"

Jut grinned at Marty. "Do you get minimum wage?"

4

"Nope. I'm sort of an extra that Doc doesn't really need, so I said I'd work for two dollars an hour. I haven't ever made that much money an hour before. Anyhow, I'd work for her for nothing."

"*I* wouldn't clean up dog poop for two dollars an hour," Nick joined in. "No way! All your clothes are gonna stink."

"Hold on a minute, troops," Mrs. Howard said. "Martin, I guess you've made your right-to-work case for now, but it's only on a trial basis. If your grades suffer, *no job*. Is that a deal?"

"Okay," Marty agreed, accepting their terms. He leaned back in his chair. *It was true what I said,* he thought. *I would work at the vet hospital for free.* Just knowing he would go straight to Old Doc every day after school made Marty feel good. Special. He had a real job. A paying job, too, although that didn't matter. Now he had somewhere important to go after school, like Jut, who always had sports or play practice or something.

Marty would be helping animals, which was certainly more special than school activities or throwing a ball around. Memories of baseball season came to mind and Marty was briefly uneasy. He loved baseball. He and Tim had been on the same baseball team every spring since second grade. But spring and baseball were a long way off. It was barely November. He would decide what to do about baseball practice when the season came around. For now, he had a job—something that no other boy in his family had.

The next morning on the way to school, Marty told Tim all about his job.

"You think Doc'll let you give shots and help with operations, and all the good stuff?" Tim asked eagerly.

Marty shook his head. "Mostly, I think I'll watch a lot, especially at first. And do the dirty work the vets don't want to do," he added, grinning. "Like John—you know, the high school kid who works there afternoons."

"Maybe," Tim agreed, "but I never heard that *he* wanted to be a real vet, and *you do.*"

Marty and Tim talked right up until the final bell, but then Marty got busy being his best school self. Whenever he had a spare moment he worked a math problem or looked up a vocabulary word in the dictionary for his English homework. He didn't waste a second. Crummy grades would mean no job, and he promised himself that he would bring his grades up. Because he was just beginning a new nine-week grading period, it was a perfect chance to show everybody how he could work and manage school, too.

"Well, guess you go one way and I go another," Tim said at the end of the school sidewalk. His voice was bleak, not excited as it had been when they had talked about the job that morning. Tim forced a smile. "You show 'em, okay, Marty?"

Marty heard all the lonely things that Tim was being so careful not to say. Slowly, he nodded as they moved apart. "Uh, Tim . . . it's just afternoons. There'll be weekends, and all day Sunday. Just like always. And some afternoon Doc won't care if you come in and keep us company. That'd be fun, wouldn't it?"

"Sure would," Tim said. "See you, now." Head down, he began walking toward home alone.

Marty watched him a minute, then sprinted down Parkview to the crossing at Grove.

I'll still see Tim a lot, Marty said to himself as his feet hurried over the sidewalk squares. *Sure I will.* He made himself keep running so that he wouldn't be late his first day at work.

7

Panting, Marty paused at the side door of the vet hospital. "Hospital Personnel Only" the sign said. *That's me,* he thought, glad and proud all over again. He sniffed barnyard manure—that unmistakable odor on the rough doormat at his feet. Nearby sat Old Doc's boots, brownly coated. She ignored manure. "That's what boots're for," he'd heard her say many times.

Inside, Marty inhaled deeply. Vet hospital smells were special and memorable. His nose filled with the rich, pungent scent of dog, along with side odors of medicine and Clorox. Cat litter blended with disinfectant. *Even blind,* Marty told himself, *I would know this place.*

The sounds were special, too. Voices came from the ever-full waiting room, where owners shared their pets' troubling symptoms or clever tricks. A boarding dog yelped repeatedly and was answered by a variety of meows, grrrs, and woofs. *Pet chorus,* Marty thought, grinning.

A woman's voice jolted him out of his absorption. "So sorry. He's always terribly scared at the vet's. Poor, poor wuzzums."

Poor wuzzums was a large sheepdog cowering at the door behind Marty. The dog had wrapped his leash around Marty's ankles, so Marty was

8

between him and his owner—a heavy, rather untidy lady.

"Here, ma'am, I'll take him." Marty unwrapped the leash and started down the hallway. But the sheepdog planted his feet and Marty, a slim eighty pounds, ground to a halt. "Were you just leaving?" he asked, hoping.

"MAXIMILIAN HARKNESS?" Old Doc's voice rang through the hospital corridors. She always called an animal into her office by its own name.

"That's us," dithered the woman. "It's our turn. Oh, poor wuzzums."

So this was Maximilian, not poor wuzzums. "Come on, Max," Marty urged.

"Here you are, Max," Doc said briskly as she rounded the corner. "Marty, I see you made it. Good for you. Bring Max into my office. Got a big day, and both Charlie and Baby Doc are on the road." Short and somewhat stocky, Old Doc whisked by Marty as she spoke.

Marty tugged on the leash and managed to drag a miserable Max across the tile floor into Doc's room. Mrs. Harkness followed, making sympathetic sounds all the way.

Old Doc pushed the button that lowered her

examining table to the floor, and all three of them heaved, trying to get Max up onto the table. Old Doc cracked Max sharply on the rump with the flat of her hand. "Right now, Max. No nonsense." And Max hauled himself onto the table.

Doc zoomed him upward with her electronic button, and Max hunkered low. "Now, what is it this time?" Old Doc asked while she ran her hands all over the dog's body. She looked into his eyes, pulled his eyelids back, opened his mouth, and peered down his throat. Max squirmed unhappily.

"He's not peppy anymore," Mrs. Harkness said. "He just eats and sleeps. No special symptoms, just not peppy."

Old Doc looked at Max's medical chart. She listened to his heart, asked Mrs. Harkness several questions, then wrote on the chart. She ran her tongue around her teeth as she thought. "Well, mainly, he's too danged prosperous. Twenty pounds overweight. Cut his food in half and take him for long walks."

Mrs. Harkness sucked in her breath. "Cut his food in *half*?"

"That's what I said. We have diet food you can

buy by the carton if you want. Call me in two weeks and let me know how you're getting on." She turned to Marty. "Don't forget the Clorox."

Vicki, the girl who worked in the office, poked her head in the door. "Doc, there's a girl on the phone wants medicine for her goats, and somebody on line two is calling about a pig."

Doc left the office. Marty pushed the button lowering Max to the floor, and reached for the Clorox bottle.

"I just don't know how he will live on such a teeny tiny amount of food," Mrs. Harkness moaned as she and the sheepdog left the room.

Marty squirted Clorox on the table and wiped carefully with paper towels. Old Doc was a stickler about sanitation. After each patient, Marty would have to wipe the table with Clorox to prevent the spread of disease, especially parvo, which Old Doc had said was so catching.

He was proud that he knew exactly what to do—that he'd been the one who had always come to Doc's office with Eleanore and Pierpont. Doc would soon see how good a worker he could be.

It was too bad Charlie and Baby Doc were on the road. Marty wanted them to know he was now part of the team. Charlie was really Dr. Charles Switzer, a vet about the age of Marty's dad. Old Doc called him Young Doc or else Charlie. Sometimes she called him Young Doc Number One, because now there was Baby Doc.

Baby Doc had been on the staff for less than a year. Like Charlie, Baby Doc had a real name. He was Hank Sullivan. Hank said he didn't mind being called Young Doc Number Two, but he resented being called Baby Doc just because he was twenty-five years old.

Marty admired all the vets. Just being around them made him feel good, and someday he would be exactly like them, he thought happily. He gave the table one last wipe.

"Put him up here," Old Doc said as she entered the room and pushed the button for the table. Two elderly men followed her in. One of the men held a thin white kitten.

"Where'd you get that kitten?" Old Doc asked.

"From a drainpipe," replied the one who held the kitten. He put it down with great tenderness on the table.

Old Doc examined the kitten. After a time she said, "Humph. Ear mites." She ran her hands over the tiny, distended stomach. "And probably roundworms." She looked into the kitten's eyes, and Marty peered over her shoulder. The eyes were blue as sky and wide with fear. Old Doc mumbled to herself.

"Clap your hands near his head," she told Marty.

Marty did as he was told. The kitten didn't budge.

"Do it again. Louder."

Marty clapped again, sadly, because he knew what Old Doc was trying to prove. "He can't hear, can he?"

Doc shook her head. "Genetic defect. White cats with blue eyes. Can't remember the exact percentage, but it's high. They're often deaf." She looked from Marty to the two old men. "This kitten's going to need care. If it isn't a house cat, it probably won't live very long."

The men moved closer together. "Then he's lucky he's got us. We don't hear so well either, huh, Ralph?"

Ralph reached his veined hand toward the kitten. "What about the ear mites . . . and the worms? We can fix that, right?" He stroked the kitten's back.

"Of course," Doc said. "He'll be good company,

too. I'll show you how to care for his ears. Mites are common in kittens. Marty, go ask Vicki for Canex for the mites and Piperazine for the roundworms." Old Doc began talking to the men about kitten shots and food, and Marty left the room.

Vicki met him in the hall. "Tell Doc there's a man on the phone wants her to make a road call on nine chickens and a turkey."

Marty nodded. Surely, this was heaven.

2.
Marty on the Job

"Take everything out of the cage," John explained to Marty the next afternoon. "Put the animal in the runs outside while you clean. This's the disinfectant. Always read the chart to see if he gets food and water or something special. If you don't read the chart every time, Doc'll have a fit."

"Got it," Marty said, as a German shepherd dragged him toward the door to the runs. "I'll be here every day now to help."

"That's great." John, a high school senior, slopped mop and disinfectant around the floor. Unlike Marty, John worked because he needed money for college expenses next fall. He was kind toward the animals, but detached.

Marty put the shepherd in the dog run and hurried back inside. Soon he had taken four dogs out, cleaned their cages, and started down Pussycat Lane, which was what John called the ward with a double row of cages reserved mainly for boarding cats. Seriously sick animals were in another wing of the hospital, close to Doc's office and the surgery.

Pussycat Lane greeted Marty with pathetic meows, playful paws reaching through bars, or ominous silence, depending on the cat.

"Hey, this one's chart says 'WILL BITE,'" Marty called to John. "How do I get her out of the cage?"

"Very carefully. If you can't do it, I'll come over and help," John answered from the next ward.

Marty wanted to do it himself. He read the cat's chart. "SABER. Mr. and Mrs. A. P. Putnam, Willow Avenue, Hampshire." The chart said how much food to give Saber and was dated five weeks back. The "WILL BITE" was stamped over everything in red letters.

Five weeks, Marty thought. *No wonder you bite.* He slowly opened the cage door. "Nice

16

kitty. It's just me, Marty. I like cats. We've got one named Eleanore. She had a whole mess of kittens and we kept her anyway."

He sneaked his hand back toward the lynx-eyed Saber, who hadn't twitched a muscle. "Kept two of her kittens, too. We named one Licky because he licks your hand all the time, just like a dog. The other one's Fishhead, a calico."

Still talking, Marty began stroking Saber's satiny-black back. He reached in with his other hand and slid it underneath Saber, who hissed, but didn't bite. "You'd like it outside, Saber. And you need to be petted, too. You're just mad because Mr. and Mrs. A. P. Putnam didn't take you with them . . . wherever they are." Marty held Saber to his chest and she was still. She didn't purr, but she allowed herself to be put outside in a pet run.

When Marty finished cleaning Saber's cage, he slid the cat back inside, still talking to her in a low voice. Saber curled up in the farthest corner and stared out at Marty accusingly.

Marty looked back at her. "I think it's mean to leave her here so long," he called to John.

Mop over his shoulder, John came around the

corner. "Ha!" he snorted. "Look at this. And this. And how about this one? Here for three months!"

Appalled, Marty read the charts as John pointed them out. "But *why*?" he exploded. "Why would anybody leave them so long? It's like prison! Cats're hunters!"

John smiled, philosophically. "Sleepers, too. They sleep most of the time. We let 'em out, and the day girls let 'em run around in the mornings. Mostly, they do okay. . . . but *I* wouldn't leave *my* cat for so long."

Marty disagreed that the cats were doing okay. When John went back to swabbing out dogs' cages, Marty took each cat prisoner out of its cage. He held them, played games with the mop trailing across the floor, and petted them. The cats, secure in Marty's big hands, purred and rubbed their heads under his chin. "I'll be back tomorrow," he promised them. The short-term boarders on Pussycat Lane got clean cages, a few quick scratches on the head, fresh water, food, and kitty litter.

"Hey, Doc," Marty said as he emerged into the main hall, "there's something I've got to talk to you about. . . . "

"Not now, Marty. There's a goat out here that's just had a kid, but her udder's not swollen with milk as it should be. She's skittish and I want you to hold her."

Marty followed her into the barnlike area that served as garage, overflow storage, and examining room for the few farm animals brought to the hospital. The goat, head down, stood by its owner and a new pickup truck.

The goat's owner perked up as Old Doc and Marty came into view. "And another thing, Doc. Minerva didn't have any afterbirth. Couldn't find it anywhere." The man held his hands out helplessly.

Old Doc showed Marty how to straddle the goat's back and hold her head while she examined the small udder for signs of milk. "The kid died, you say?" She squeezed the goat's teats and a weak stream of milk spurted out.

"This her first kid?" Doc asked.

The man nodded. "Mine, too. Never had goats before. Of course, we never had any place in the city. We didn't even know she was with kid. Now it's dead. And no afterbirth, like I said."

"You didn't find her for a while, so she probably ate the afterbirth. But we'll check to be sure." Doc stood up and massaged her back tiredly. "Marty, tell Vicki I need a syringe and some pituitary extract. We can bring the milk in with that, I hope. Bring me a rubber glove and some liquid antiseptic in a pan."

Marty got the supplies while Old Doc talked to the man who had never had goats before. When he returned, the man was saying, "But how do you know a goat's pregnant?"

Doc smiled. "You know your goat's going to have a kid when she presents you with one." She turned to Marty. "Hold her again, like before, and I'll go fishing for that afterbirth."

She pulled the paper off a sterile glove, then slopped her gloved hand in the liquid antiseptic before reaching deep inside the female goat. Her face had an air of intense concentration as she felt for the tissue that had once nourished the lost kid.

Embarrassed, Marty turned his head around. He stared down at Minerva's nose and tried not to hear her when she bleated unhappily. The goat danced, eager to get away, but he held on tight. He told himself that putting your hand up inside a goat was routine. Everyday work for a vet. He just hadn't thought about it before.

"Nope. Clean as a whistle. Minerva's had a bad go of it this time, but next time should be better. She'll probably have more kids." Doc peeled off the rubber glove, then swiftly gave Minerva her injection of pituitary extract.

"Okay, Marty, we can get her into the pickup. You go Clorox my table and I'll be right in."

In the hallway, Marty saw Young Doc Number One and Baby Doc talking. He stopped next to them. "Hi. Did you guys know I'm working here now?"

Charlie Switzer clapped Marty on the shoulder. "Welcome to the loony bin. You must need money pretty badly. Right, Hank?"

Dr. Hank Sullivan grinned. "Marty knows this job isn't for money. How's Pierpont's hind leg? Less stiff?"

"Lots better. Those're some shots. You said he couldn't have very many. Why's that?"

Dr. Switzer spoke. "They're pretty strong. He's old enough that we don't really worry, but it's hospital policy to give cortisone only when necessary." He excused himself and went into his examining room.

"Pierpont's not old, only fourteen. Some dogs live lots longer than that." Concerned, Marty looked at Hank.

Hank turned toward his room and motioned for Marty to follow. "Remember that Pierpont's first two years are like twenty-one years for humans. Then add four years for every year after that. So how old does that make Pierpont?"

Marty added it up. "Makes him sixty-nine years old. But I thought it was seven years for every human year. Geez, that would be worse."

Hank nodded. "This way of reckoning is supposed to be more accurate. Any way you figure, though, Pierpont's an old pooch." He put medicine bottles into a tiny office refrigerator as he talked.

"He's part of our family. He's just like the first baby, Dad says, because they got him right after Jut was born."

Hank wiped a set of fur trimmers. "Yes, but remember, our pets are only on loan to us for a little time, Marty. Like the colored leaves in the fall." He put the trimmers in a drawer. "Know what I mean?"

Marty knew, although he didn't like knowing. He couldn't imagine their family without funny old Pierpont.

"You ought to come on the road with me sometime, Marty. I'd like the company, and Old Doc won't care."

"Yeah, sure. Thanks a lot. I'd like to work with big animals . . . I think." Marty hesitated. "But something's bugging me. You know those cats in Ward One?" Ward One was the real name for Pussycat Lane.

"Which cats?"

"The ones that've been here *forever*. One's been here three months and it's only a kitten!"

Hank stopped straightening his office. "Well, they're healthy, or they were last time I checked. Can't be very happy, though. Is that what you mean?"

"Sure. It's not natural for them in cages. I think we should call their owners."

"That's up to Old Doc."

"I'll talk to her about it." Marty went out into the hall. "But I'd like to go on the road some Saturday, Hank. Can I call you Hank?"

"Anything but 'Baby Doc,' " he replied. "See you around."

When Marty found Old Doc, she was pouring disinfectant into an ugly wound in the haunch of a white rabbit. He remembered that he hadn't Cloroxed the table.

"Forgot the table," he mumbled as he slid past her into the corner of the room.

"So you did. Hand me a syringe and that white bottle next to the refrigerator and take Molly out of here. Says she's going to be sick."

Marty took Molly into the waiting room. She was small and frightened, and beside her Marty felt old. "What happened to your rabbit?" he asked, hoping she wouldn't be sick.

"The neighbor's dog got her. Is she going to die?"

Marty swallowed. "I don't know. Old Doc'll save your rabbit if she can, I know that." He thought of what Hank had just told him—that animals were lent to people for only a short time. But he couldn't say that to this girl, not now. So he sat next to her and was quiet.

Several minutes passed before Old Doc brought the rabbit to the waiting room. "You bring Pansy back in five days and let me examine her wound. Her leg will be sore, so be careful of it and keep it clean. Put these drops into the wound every day just like it says in these instructions." She handed the instructions over along with the rabbit.

Marty followed Old Doc back toward the examining room. She detoured on the way to show him a dark-brown, curly-haired guinea pig in a box in the surgery. "A man just left him here at the front desk. Said his children didn't want him anymore and we're supposed to put him to sleep, but I hate to. He's only two years old. Know anyone who wants an expensive Peruvian long-haired guinea pig?"

"Put him to sleep?" Marty croaked. "Is he sick?"

"Perfectly healthy. They don't want him anymore. If I kept every animal nobody wants, we'd be overrun. If you want to try to find him a home, I'll keep him here a few days."

Marty spoke quickly. "I'll take him. Nick would love him, and Mom won't care . . . I hope."

"Okay by me. I have to run. Got two road calls before supper. See you tomorrow, and don't forget to Clorox my table before you go."

In the November twilight Marty walked home. He had forgotten to tell Old Doc about the cats that had been boarders for too long a time. Tomorrow, they would have to talk about what to do for them.

And now he had a pet nobody wanted, who would die if he couldn't convince his family—or somebody's family—to keep it. He peeked in at the guinea pig, who shifted around in his box and looked up at him with liquid eyes as he made a squeaking sound. Marty held the box tighter.

He thought about his second afternoon at the vets' hospital, and decided that heaven had a smudge on it.

3.

Vet Routine

Marty opened the box to show his mother what quivered inside it. He chose his words carefully.

"He's a very rare, expensive, Peruvian long-haired guinea pig. Can I give him to Nick? Nine's old enough to take care of a pet, and he doesn't know I have it. I wanted to be sure you approved first, okay?"

Mrs. Howard looked from the furry little pig to Marty and back to the pig. She stopped peeling potatoes. "What happens if I say no?"

"He dies. The people that had him don't want him anymore. A man brought him in to be put to sleep."

"I thought so. Martin, this is going to happen

all the time. We can't adopt every orphan that finds its way to the vets' office. You know that, son."

"I've been thinking about it all the way home! But Nick doesn't have a pet of his own. The kittens play with everybody, Pierpont's too old, and Eleanore's yours. I know we can't take in all the strays, but couldn't we take this one, this one time? Look at him—he's too young to die!" Marty shoved the box under his mother's face again.

Mrs. Howard nodded slowly. "Okay. You got me this time, but I'm serious, Marty. We can't keep adopting strays. Only your second day at the vets', and already we have a new pet. But *no more.*"

A small voice in Marty's head asked him what he was going to do the next time an animal needed rescuing. He told the small voice to shut up.

As soon as Nick came home from his friend Billy's house, Marty handed him the box. Naturally nervous, the unsettled guinea pig began squeaking. Nick shouted with excitement and the uproar woke Pierpont, who insisted on nosing into Nick's new box. Pierpont snuffled the terrified pig, looked at Nick with disgust, and ambled back to his comfortable rug.

But Nick thought the guinea pig the best present he'd ever had and told Marty so several times. He clutched the small animal tightly to his chest. "Wait'll I tell Billy I've got a Peruvian long-haired guinea pig!" he exulted.

"I want it, Nick. I want it." Gus pulled on Nick's T-shirt and reached up for the furry animal.

"Okay, Gus, okay." Marty took the pig and held it out for Gus. "We'd better let him pet it, Nick, or he'll have a fit. Then Mom'll be sorry she said you could keep him."

At suppertime, Nick kept his pig in its box under his chair. Eleanore pawed at the box until she, too, was allowed to inspect the new family member. Eleanore thought she'd like to play with the pig, but Nick protectively closed the box. "No, no, Eleanore! Your claws're sharp and you look hungry." He pushed Eleanore away. "I better put him in an old aquarium quick before she gets him," Nick announced.

"She could, too," Jut said. "Guinea pigs are dumb, you know. You should name him Gooney Pig," he teased.

Surprisingly, Nick agreed. "I know, that's

why he needs me to protect him. Poor Gooney Pig," he said lovingly, bending over to check the safety of his pet one more time.

Phew! Marty thought, relieved. He had never let himself believe that the guinea pig would be turned away from their home, but the annoying small voice in his head had known it could happen. Marty was quiet as he ate.

"Must be a very thought-provoking job," his dad teased. "Or a very solemn one." He forked in a mouthful of peas.

"No, no!" protested Marty. "It's fun. The time just flies by. And Old Doc lets me help a lot." He launched into a detailed description of how helpful he was on the job.

"Poor nanny goat," his mother said on hearing the tale of the goat and her lost kid.

"Cleaning out dog cages! Dog poop, just like I said," Nick exclaimed triumphantly.

"Not at the table, Nicholas," scolded Mrs. Howard.

"Can I have more ribs?" Gus asked.

Jut passed the plate of barbecued ribs to Gus. "Don't take all of them, okay?" He turned to Marty. "Have you made any money—I mean, real money?"

"Ten dollars. In two measly afternoons. Put

that in your pipe and smoke it," he said, repeating an old phrase that Mr. Howard liked to use. Jut opened his mouth to retort.

"*Can it*, boys! Marty's just started this job." Mr. Howard spoke in his firmest voice. "If you're interested in what goes on at the vets' office, fine. But no negative talk. Get me?"

"Did *I* say anything negative?" Jut asked, insulted.

Mrs. Howard shook her head. "No, Jut, that isn't what your father meant. It's just that we should all be supportive of Marty in his new job. Now, who would like ice cream for dessert?"

That night Marty had trouble concentrating on his homework. His science class was learning to write lab reports, and his report was on a mouse experiment they'd done. The mice had been in cages, of course. But now, when he saw the word *cages*, he thought of the cat boarders he'd met that day.

The finished lab report was less than perfect. It had words crossed out here and there and blots in noticeable places. Marty put it into his notebook anyway and got ready for bed. When Jut came back from his shower, Marty wanted to talk to him—to see how Jut felt about boarding animals a long time.

Wednesday afternoon was the vets' regular afternoon on the road, so office hours were not kept. Marty went to work anyway, and helped John clean cages. Then he played catch-the-mop with the long-term cat boarders, took them outdoors, and petted them. When he left, they meowed him out the door.

He felt a bit better about the cats that day. Jut had told him he was too involved with Old Doc's business. Marty had told Jut it was *his* business, too.

When Marty came to work Thursday, the volume of woofs, growls, and yips told him it was a dog day. He peeked in at the waiting room, jammed with dogs and owners. One time he had taken Eleanore to see Old Doc, and nearly all the patients that day had been cats.

"LUCKY, WHEATSTRAW, MAJOR, AND PRINCESS NEWTON?" boomed Old Doc's voice right behind him. "Hi, Marty. Help the Newtons in with their dogs."

Borne on a tide of dogs, Mr. and Mrs. Newton advanced toward Marty and Old Doc. All four people and four dogs surged down the hall and through the doorway into the examining room. Marty shut the door, turned around, and pressed himself flat against it. There was nowhere else to go. The small room was as full as it could get.

Each of the dogs was examined and treated. Lucky, a shimmering golden retriever, was a stray the Newtons had found years ago crouched on the railroad tracks in Cincinnati. All the dogs had been adopted as strays, Marty learned.

The fawn-colored Labrador had been left on a farm where she had hidden in the straw, and so had been christened Wheatstraw.

Major, a three-legged German shepherd, had been found on a street corner one winter night. His left foreleg, now gone, had been injured. "By a car accident, mebee," volunteered Mr. Newton. He rubbed the shepherd's head. "We brought him here, and Old Doc amputated his leg that night."

Princess, the last and largest, was a black Newfoundland and the biggest dog Marty had ever been in a very small room with. She was also the calmest, and nearly went to sleep on the table. When Old Doc gave her her vaccination, Princess just yawned.

"Well, Marty, smell anything?" Old Doc looked at him expectantly.

Marty sniffed. He sniffed again, pushed his glasses into place, and said, "No. Nothing." In a room this crammed with dog, he ought to smell dog.

"Ha!" Doc chortled. "The Newtons are vegetarians. So are their dogs. Maybe that's why they never have a doggy odor. Isn't it wonderful?" Doc stroked Princess's glossy black coat.

Marty agreed it was wonderful not to smell dog multiplied times four. Their visit over, the six Newtons exploded into the hall, and out the doors that Marty and Vicki held open for them.

"Where'd Doc go?" Vicki asked. "There's a lady on the phone. Her kid saw this ball of peanut butter on the counter and ate it. Only it was the dog's heartworm pill—dog won't take it any other way—and this mom's about to self-destruct."

When Marty told Doc about the phone emergency, she smiled. "Some kid eats dog food or dog medicine all the time. Luckily, this one isn't serious. Most times it isn't. I'll go talk to her."

"Just a second, Doc—could we talk about those cats?" Hurriedly, Marty explained about the prisoners of Pussycat Lane. "So we've got to call their owners, don't you think? Boots is just a kitten. He's hardly ever played in the grass!"

Doc put her hand on Marty's shoulder. "I know what you're trying to say, Marty. And it's because you care about animals that I have you working here. But don't worry unless worry is needed. Those owners all have good reasons. One's out of the country, another's ill, and so on, but their cats are healthy so far. That's our job—keeping the animals healthy. I'll watch them, I promise."

Reluctantly, Marty nodded. She was the boss. "How about if I take them for walks on leashes?"

"Don't know that cats appreciate leashes, but you can try. Now you get our next patient and do the table while I take that phone call."

Marty did the Clorox act and picked up the chart for the next patient. In the doorway of the waiting room, wishing he had a white coat like all the vets, he boomed, "HANNIBAL GREEN?"

Hannibal Green, surprisingly, was not a dog like all the other patients this Thursday. He was a large, ginger-colored, Morris kind of cat that Marty liked immediately. "He ought to be in commercials," Marty told the boy carrying Hannibal.

"You Nick's brother?" the boy asked. "You got any more guinea pigs like Gooney? He came to school today with Nick."

"No more guinea pigs, sorry. Your cat Hannibal—he isn't sick, is he?"

"He's gonna be," the boy said gloomily. "Mom says we gotta get him nootered. He howls at night and squirts smelly stuff. Today he squirted Mom's car."

Marty grinned. "Put him up here on Doc's table. Doc, this is Hannibal Green. He's come to be an *it*."

Doc examined the cat to be sure he was healthy. "Do you want to watch his operation?" she asked the boy.

He shook his head. "I'll wait in the waiting room. There're puppies out there. I brought a box to take him home in. Mom said he'd be all dopey."

"He'll be under anaesthetic for several hours. I'll write instructions for you and your mother and bring him out to you when he's finished."

The boy hesitated at the door. "It won't hurt, will it? I'll know if he meows loud that it's hurting."

"He won't feel a thing." Doc injected anaesthetic into Hannibal's rear end. "See? He's going to sleep already."

When Hannibal's owner was gone, Doc handed the relaxed and sagging form of the cat to Marty. "Okay, now we'll go put him on the rack."

"That sounds awful," Marty said, following her down the hall to the surgery.

In the surgery stood a waist-high stainless steel sink. Balanced across its top was a long stainless steel rack that looked like the one his mother set cake pans on to cool before she frosted the cake. At Doc's direction, he laid Hannibal out on the rack.

"Aren't his eyes going to close? That's creepy."

"No, they'll stay open because he's unconscious. His reflexes don't work when he's not conscious, so he can't close his eyes. But he won't feel a thing." She got out a set of fur trimmers and trimmed all the fur from Hannibal's testicle area.

Then she sprayed warm water and soap on the area and scrubbed. She rinsed the cat and followed the washing with a liberal douse of orangey-red disinfectant. "Now he's sterile," Doc said.

Marty averted his eyes. His face was growing pinker by the minute and he couldn't stop it. *Why hadn't he thought of these things?* Here he was, with Old Doc—a woman, for cripes' sake— helping to castrate a cat. He couldn't remember when he had been this embarrassed.

Old Doc looked up and saw Marty's face. "This is a marvelous operation," she announced. "Prevents all kinds of unwanted kittens in Hampshire, and we've got more than our share as it is. Neutering a cat is one of my favorite activites. Let's see how fast I can do it. Start timing now, and I'll tell you when to stop. Okay, go!"

Gratefully, Marty set the stopwatch on the new watch he'd gotten for his twelfth birthday. And then, because his curiosity wouldn't go away, he watched the veterinarian's hands.

In one swift motion, Doc slit the skin around one testicle, then the other, and each was freed from its skin sac. She pulled the testicles forward. "This is the vas deferens." She pointed to a tiny tube that looked like a cord. "It carries the sperm from the testicle to the urethra—here.

Only now, it will have nowhere to go." She tied the two cords and snipped each testicle free.

That done, she swabbed more antiseptic all over Hannibal's shaved area. "Doesn't bleed enough to notice. No stitches needed either. And now he can ignore lady cats.

"Quick, Marty, stop! How long was that?"

"Two minutes and five seconds." He looked up from his watch. "That's great! Uh, do you . . . do you hold the office record?" He was determined to treat this as casually as Doc did.

"You'll have to time Charlie and Baby Doc. I know I can beat Baby Doc, but I'm not sure about Charlie."

She picked up Hannibal and stroked his furry length. "Beautiful coat. They must be giving him brewer's yeast. Marty, be sure to remind me to tell cat owners about brewer's yeast." Doc moved toward the door. "Some vets keep castrated cats overnight, but not me. Too many germs handy here, in spite of all our cleaning. He'll do better at home."

Marty nodded and started to clean up the sink and rack. "See you tomorrow, Doc."

Next time will be easier, he thought, hosing down the sink. *Neutering animals is probably a big part of vet practice. I'd have known that if I'd just thought about it.*

Guess I'll go pet pussycats, he decided, looking at the door that led to Ward One.

4.

One-Man Rescue Squad

On the lawn outside the veterinary hospital, Marty coaxed the cats. "Come on! Don't sit there like stumps! Dogs go on leashes, so why not you?"

Two of the long-term boarders crouched on the grass at Marty's feet and refused to budge. The large calico female, Gretchen, looked miserably up at Marty. Samson, the male, looked at his paws. Neither would go anywhere.

Marty tried pulling on the leashes. Next, he set Gretchen on her feet and pushed, encouraging her to walk. After two steps, Gretchen plumped herself down again. Samson kept looking at his paws. When Marty pulled on his leash,

Samson planted himself in the grass.

Disgusted, Marty took them inside. "They hate leashes," he told Vicki when he saw her in the office.

"Yup. I tried walking cats, too, couple years back. You could try the younger one, though."

But the little cat named Boots was no different. Like Samson, he hunkered low and looked down at his paws or the grass. He didn't look gratefully at Marty and he didn't prance happily at the end of the leash.

"Guess I won't even try Saber," Marty muttered to himself as he put Boots back in his cage. He had spent some time with the satiny Saber earlier. She now let him handle her without hissing, but she never purred or rubbed against his leg. He imagined smoldering anger in her lynx eyes, but he hadn't felt it. The card on her cage still had "WILL BITE" stamped on it in red ink.

Vicki called down Ward One. "Doc wants you in surgery, Marty. Emergency." She left, running to answer the office phone.

Marty hustled into the surgery with a pounding heart. Emergency. And Doc wanted him.

She looked up as Marty burst through the

swinging doors of the surgery. "Good boy. You hold this cat in place while I tie her to the table." She gestured at a dainty, silky-gray cat drifting into anaesthetized sleep.

Marty put his hands around the cat as Doc tied the cords around each hind leg to hooks on the underside of the small-animal operating table. The cat's forelegs were already pinned under a metal restraining bar. "What's the problem?"

"Uterus full of dead kittens, I suspect. She had one kit stillborn two days ago and never delivered the rest."

Marty blinked. "*Two days ago?* What'd they *wait* for?"

Old Doc shook her head. "Who knows? We'll try, but I think it's hopeless. I want you to watch to make sure her heart doesn't stop beating, okay? She seems weak to me."

Immediately Marty's gaze was drawn to the cat's gently heaving chest. Thump, thump. It was beating now. He watched the small chest as though the cat's life depended on his never looking away. That was how he felt. If he looked away, even for an instant, the cat would die.

After several minutes, Doc spoke. "Relax,

Marty, I'm doing all I can. Luckily, a mother cat can go on just as before, as though nothing had happened. Animals are wonderful that way. Yup, here they are." Old Doc held up the uterus, a Y-shaped organ, bulging now with the litter that had never been born.

Marty tore his eyes away from the mother cat's chest and looked at what Doc was showing him.

"Are . . . are they dead? You're sure we can't revive any of them?"

"I'm sure. But the mother is doing fine. She has a family who loves her, so her life will go on as before." Doc put the full uterus into the steel garbage pail that always sat at the foot of the operating table.

Horrified, Marty watched her discard the kittens. "How can you talk this way?" he exploded. "It's all their fault! If they'd brought her in right away, after the first one was born, we could have done a cesarean!" He looked not at the vet, but down into the pail.

Old Doc stood up from her stool to get a better angle as she examined the open abdomen of the cat. "Remember, Marty, that the first one was born dead. The mother gave up then, and nature usually knows best. Perhaps something was wrong with the entire litter."

"Maybe. But I still say it's a crime!"

"Hand me that white package. Now tear it open lengthwise. I can reach in to get the gut." She poked fingers through the narrow opening to pull out the fine gut she used to sew the inner layers of abdominal muscle. She sewed several stitches, while Marty watched and thought.

"It's not near as bloody as I thought it'd be," Marty said. He had expected quarts of red blood all over the place.

"Let's hope not. Lots of blood means I goofed."

"I still say this operation's a crime," he repeated stubbornly.

Bent over her work, Old Doc nodded as much as to say she agreed with him. "Yes, but a vet can't reform the world. This cat was brought here to be saved, and chances are we'll do it. Not long ago, she'd have died with those kittens inside her."

She stopped stitching and looked up. "You care too much, Marty. Put your emotions aside, if you want to be a vet. You do what you can— the best you can—every day. Hand me that blue package, please. I'm ready to close up. How's her heart?"

Guiltily, Marty looked back at the cat's chest. He'd forgotten his job. "Okay," he said, relieved. He gave her the blue package.

"Tear it open like the other one. This's stainless steel for external stitches. Doesn't irritate the tissues. And"—she grinned—"I can find it again when I need to take those stitches out." With her wrist she moved her gold-rimmed glasses upward on her nose. Then she concentrated on stitching, making the stainless steel wire behave as though it were ordinary sewing thread. A row of tidy, knotted, shiny stitches appeared in the center of the cat's lower abdomen.

Marty watched the heartbeat and stitching and thought about what Doc had said. A vet couldn't reform the world and he wasn't allowed to care, at least not very much. How hard and unfeeling that sounded. Yet Doc was neither of those things.

"You care," he said finally. "That's why you're so good. And Dr. Switzer and Hank, too. Everybody knows it. That's why they come here."

Old Doc tied off the last steely knot. "True. But we know our limitations, and they are many. An animal can't tell us where it hurts or how it hurts. We guess a lot, Marty. We have to; it's the nature of the business. And if we let ourselves care too much about every mistake, we'd be destroyed. Then how much good could we do?"

He saw her truth. "You . . . you wall yourself off, then? On purpose?"

"Yessir. On purpose, and it's the first lesson." She pulled off her rubber gloves and dropped them into the pail at her feet before looking again at Marty. "And maybe the hardest lesson. Remember it. You'll need it here."

Doc untied the sleeping cat and handed her to Marty. "Put her in Ward Three where I can watch her. I'll make out the chart, and you help John clean cages. Charlie and Baby Doc must have taken care of most of the patients. Thanks, Marty."

"See you tomorrow, Doc." He put the now-slender, silky cat into a cage, placing her tenderly on a clean terrycloth towel. Then he joined John in Ward Two, where all the dogs were.

"Do that sheltie over there, Marty. He's dancing around like he has to mess his cage and I'd just as soon he messed the dog run." John scrubbed at the inside of another cage.

As they worked, Marty told John about the operation he had just assisted. "So the mother cat lost every one of them," he finished. "Every single one."

John shook his head in sympathy. "I've seen that happen. But I'm afraid there's no shortage of cats . . . or dogs, either. See those three pups at the end there? They've been here over two months now and nobody wants them. I've had a sign up in the waiting room, but here they are. Charlie says we'll take them to the pound now and give up."

Marty leaned his mop against the wall and went to look at the puppies. They were what his mother called Heinz 57, a mixed breed. No fancy pedigree to guarantee them homes. Not like Wellington's Highborn Lady, an expensive wolf-hound puppy who'd recently been a patient.

"They're awful cute," Marty said as one furry brown pup licked his hand. "And friendly." He reached through the bars to scratch each one behind its ears. "Will they be adopted better from the pound than from here?"

"Nah. Probably be put to sleep." John did not look at Marty.

Marty looked hard at the appealing puppies,

then looked away. He tried walling himself off from the awful words John had said. "How'd they *get* here? Why do *we* have to take them to the pound?"

"Somebody just left them here in a box. There were four of them, only one died right away. We give away lots of animals, all the time, that people just dump here. It's a real pain."

It sure is, Marty fumed. *And a crime, too, like those poor kittens in surgery. It's too much.*

"I'll find them homes," Marty announced. He wasn't sure where or how, but he knew he would do it. "I'll take them with me tonight when I go."

John leaned on his mop and just looked at Marty. He didn't say anything.

"Well, you can't take them to the pound *knowing*!" Marty backed up against the cage that housed the orphan pups. "Anyway, I can't!"

"We can't keep them all either, or there'd be no room for the sick ones. They cost a lot to feed."

"I'll find them homes," repeated Marty.

John shrugged his shoulders and went back to mopping. "There'll be more, you know," he said with his back to Marty. "There'll always be more."

Marty closed his eyes. "I know. But right now

there're only three. That's not very many. Lots of people in Hampshire don't have pets, and I'll bet they'd like one."

"You can probably convince them if anyone can," John admitted, smiling and shaking his head. "But before you ask me, the answer's no. My mom'd throw me out of the house if I brought home one more animal. We've got two cats, a bird, and a dog now."

"Well, that's more like it," Marty replied. "If more people had homes like yours, and mine, we wouldn't have this problem."

"Go get that sheltie, Marty. We'll never finish at this rate."

That evening, the twilight found Marty walking home with another box—this one bigger and squirming with three active puppies. He had been hesitant walking home with the guinea pig. This time he was determined. He would find homes for the homeless if it was the last thing he ever did. These puppies deserved better from the world.

Except—his mother probably didn't need to know about them.

5.
Martin Howard & Company, Puppy Salesmen

"There's *what* in the closet?" Jut's voice rose to a horrified squeak. He hated it when his voice did that.

"Sssh, Jut, geez! I wouldn't have put them there if I hadn't wanted to keep it a secret."

"What's a secret?" Nick had burst into the room after the briefest of knocks.

"Did he knock?" Marty asked Jut.

"Sorta. Look, Nick, we can't talk to you now."

Suddenly Marty shook his head. For once, Nick might be helpful—and Nick owed him one, after getting Gooney Pig. "Hey, Nick? You want to help us with a very special, very secret project? I mean, Top Secret."

"Sure. I can help—only you guys never let

me." Nick's dark brown eyes were as serious as his voice.

"You can't tell anybody, not even Mom and Dad."

Jut nodded. "Especially not Mom and Dad."

Marty explained to Nick about the three orphan puppies, doomed to the pound if they, the Howard family, didn't find them homes.

Nick's eyes sparkled. "Bet that box's a mess by now. Do you know how often puppies have to poo—"

"Don't think about that, Nick," interrupted Jut. "Just think about who might like to have a puppy. Who do you know in fourth grade who wants a dog?"

Nick frowned with concentration. "Nobody. But somebody might take one for a few days, until we found real homes."

Marty and Jut looked at Nick with respect. "Nick," Marty said warmly, "I never had a better idea. We can just put them any old place for now, and promise that we'll find permanent homes in a few days."

At that moment, a shrill yelping came from inside the closet. A few yaps followed, then a puppy growl.

"Can I see 'em?" Nick begged.

The bedroom door opened again, and Gus came in. "I want to see the doggy."

Jut, Marty, and Nick groaned in unison. Gus was a good kid for a four-year-old brother, but he was stubborn beyond belief. Once he got his mind fixed on something, no one could deter him.

Before anyone downstairs could hear the puppies again, Marty shut the door and switched on his radio. He smiled down at Gus. "No dog, Gus. Sorry."

"But I want to see the doggy." Gus moved toward the closet, glancing around the room as he went.

Jut leaped off the bed and stood in front of their closet. "*No dog,* Gus. Nick was just practicing for his part in a class play, *weren't you, Nick?*"

Nick jerked his head up and down and said, "Yeah, yeah," several times. "Wanta hear me, Gus?" Without waiting, Nick erupted into a series of yips, barks, and growls.

Answering yips, barks, and growls came from the closet. From downstairs, Pierpont's deep woof rose clearly.

Marty turned up the radio.

"Aaaaooooooo," howled Jut, throwing his head back.

"Rowr, rowr, rowr!" barked Marty. "Rowr! Rowr!"

"Yowlp, yowwlp!" Nick's shrill yelps rose above the rest. "Hrrr, hrrrrr, hrrrr," he added.

Gus stood back and watched his older brothers. They had never acted this way before. It looked like fun. "Ooof, ooof," he tried, imitating Pierpont. "Ooof, ooof!"

A brisk pounding on the door stopped everyone.

"BOYS! BOYS! WHAT IN HEAVEN'S NAME IS GOING ON IN THERE?"

Marty turned the radio down, but only a little. "Open the door, Jut, or we've had it."

Jut opened the door a crack and peeked around. "Animal chorus?" he said. "Pretty good, hunh?"

Mrs. Howard did not try to enter. "What *are* you doing? And how can you stand that music so loud?" By her feet stood Pierpont, nose twitching. "Ooof!" he added forcefully.

Gus came to the crack in the door and looked out at his mother. "I came to see the doggy," he said.

"Just practicing, Mom," Jut broke in. "Nick's going to be a dog in a class play, and we're helping him to get it right."

"He is? He didn't tell me. Nick, when is your play? I should put it on my calendar, so I can be sure to be there."

Nick joined the crowd at the crack in the door. He managed to ease Gus out into the hallway with their mother and Pierpont. "It's . . . it's not for sure yet. We're just fooling around with it, sorta. But if it gets good, then I'll let you know, okay?"

Looking confused, Mrs. Howard said, "All right, Nick. But you finish rehearsing soon because supper's almost ready. Is Marty in there?"

Marty had been silently congratulating Nick on being a born liar. He snapped to attention. "Yeah, Mom?"

"Come down in five or ten minutes to set the table, please."

"Be right there," Marty sang out. "Take Gus with you, okay?"

Mrs. Howard left, taking Gus and Pierpont. Even above the music they could hear him telling her something about a doggy.

Jut shut the door and leaned against it. "Marty, we have to get those puppies out of here and it's suppertime already. What're we going to do?" He paused. "And how did I get into this?"

Marty smiled at him. "Because that's what big brothers are for."

Jut moaned, but Marty could tell that he was pleased anyway.

"I think Jason Markham'll take one," Nick said loudly over the radio.

"That's too far away," Marty protested.

"Let me call him on Mom's phone and see," Nick urged. "If he says yes, that's one. Isn't that good?"

"Sure, Nick," Marty agreed hastily. "Great, but . . . you gave me *another* idea, too. I should call Tim. Let me quick call him, okay? Then you can call Jason."

Marty oozed carefully out his door and tiptoed down to his parents' room and the telephone. "Hello, Tim?" he whispered.

"Why're you whispering?" Tim asked, as if there had been no break between the time they had talked during school and now.

"Sssh," Marty breathed into the receiver. "I have to keep this a secret. *You do too,* okay?"

"Gotcha," Tim breathed back. "What is it?"

"I brought home some puppies from the vet that nobody wants, and I just need a baby-sitter for one until I find it a real home. Can you do it? Just for a few days?"

"What're you going to do with the others?"

Marty sighed impatiently. Somebody, like his mother, was going to find him here if he didn't hurry up. "Find other sitters, Tim. Quick! Can you take one of them or not?"

Marty listened to silence. Finally, Tim whispered, "I don't know how, Marty. Where would I put it? All we've got is a carport. We don't even have a shed, and Golda'd smell one out for sure if I tried to keep it in the house. You know how retrievers are about smelling things."

Marty knew Tim was right. "It's okay, Tim, forget it. I'll find somebody. See you in school tomorrow."

"Wait!" Tim hissed into the phone. "Check out Ruthann. She's close, and they've got that old barn. And Rusty's got the pool shed way out back, remember?"

"Great!" cheered Marty, forgetting about his need to whisper. "Great," he said again, very softly. "I've got to go. Talk to you tomorrow." Marty hung up and snuck back down the hall to his room where Nick, Jut, and the puppies waited.

"Well?" Jut said, as soon as Marty slipped through the door.

"No dice with Tim, but he had two terrific ideas. Ruthann has that big old barn where she could keep one, and Rusty has the pool shed, and it's way far away from their house."

"Can I call Jason now?" Nick asked.

"Right now," Jut said. "And if he says yes, I'll go with you to Markhams'."

"You just wanta see Gwen Markham," Nick teased.

"Shut up, Nick," Jut said in his touchiest voice. "Any more of that and you can't help."

Marty rushed to calm them down. "Nick won't say anything more. And we all have to help, so let's not argue. Nick, you call Jason, and make sure nobody listens in."

"I think the best way is to just *go to their houses,*" Jut insisted after Nick had gone to the phone. "It's hard to turn down a live puppy, but it'd be easy to say no on the phone."

"Right. Now how are we going to get out of the house after supper? It's dark and cold." Worriedly, Marty pushed his glasses into place and ran a hand through his wavy brown hair. He wished he had thought all of this out on the way home.

Jut ran a hand through his own hair. He chewed absentmindedly on one lip while he thought. "A game of flashlight tag. Over at Holly Tree Court."

Instantly Marty saw how right it was. It got them out of the house, with flashlights, and out of their own yard. "With a brother like you," Marty said, "I don't even have to think."

"I've noticed."

Contented, Marty let him win the point. The main thing was to get the puppies into good homes. That was all that was important.

Nick bounded into the room. "I knew it!"

"Jason'll take one?" Marty and Jut asked with one voice.

"Yup. See, his mom has this little teensy dog named Dinki, and his sister Gwen has a cat, really pretty cat, too, and so he thinks if he tells them about the puppy—after a few days—they might let him keep it. And for sure they won't care if he just kinda baby-sits it awhile."

"Great! You and Jut can go right after supper."

When supper was over, Jut encouraged his parents to go into the living room while he and Marty cleaned up the dishes. After they'd gone, Marty sent Nick upstairs to get the box of puppies. "Take them to the garage, Nick. They'll be okay till we get there. And don't let *anyone* see you coming downstairs!"

Nick smuggled the puppy box down the steps and into the garage. When he got back into the house, he found Marty and whispered in his ear, "All systems go. Fire rockets."

Marty got their flashlights out, tested them to see if they worked, and went into the living room. "Hi, there," he said, feeling more than a little foolish.

Mr. Howard looked up from the book he was reading. He leaned over to poke the logs in the fireplace. "Hi, yourself. What are the flashlights for?"

"Just a little game of flashlight tag, okay?"

"Flashlight tag?" asked his mother. "I am working on our Thanksgiving menu and you're going outdoors to play tag? One of us is crazy."

"Last game of the season," Marty said firmly. "Everybody wanted one last game and my homework's done. Won't be long. 'Bye." His homework wasn't done, but he felt he needed a strong case and he could always do his homework later.

"Wear your hats, then, and don't be gone long.

Are you going over to Holly Tree Court?"

"Just like always." He waved a flashlight in the air and left before they changed their minds.

In the garage, Marty found Jut and Nick playing with the puppies. "Boy, are they nice," Nick said. "I wish we could keep one."

"Forget it." Jut stood up. "Come on, Nick. We'll put that one with the black ears and tail into this box and take him to Markhams'. He's the cutest, so maybe they'll keep him, like you said." Jut loaded the wriggly puppy into the box, and they started toward the garage door.

"Wait!" Marty called. "We have to meet at the Court and come home together. What time is it?"

"Seven o'clock. How about meeting in an hour? Any longer and the folks'll call over there and then we're in trouble."

Marty waved them off. He picked up his box of two puppies and went as fast as he could down the driveway, through three backyards, and then down Willow Avenue to Ruthann's house.

On Ruthann's porch, he prayed that she, and not her gramma, would answer the doorbell.

She did. "Hi, Marty, what're you doing here?"

Marty was caught off guard by her directness. "Uh, I've got this terrible problem, Ruthann, and I was sure you could help."

"Come inside. It's cold out here."

"No, no," Marty said. "I'll be quick. About this problem, Ruthann. I work at Old Doc's vet hospital now, did you know that?"

Shivering, Ruthann shook her head no. "Get to the point, Marty!"

"I'm getting, I'm getting!" He took a deep breath. "The puppies in this box are going to die if we don't save them."

Ruthann backed away from him. "No you don't, Marty Howard. No way! We can hardly feed ourselves, and that's that. I can't have a pet, no way."

"Not to keep! Just to, well, to baby-sit until I find him a permanent home. Or her. I don't know what I've got. One of them's already gone to Markhams'. Jason's going to try to keep him, but we don't know for sure. I've got two left. You can have whichever one you want—only you don't have to keep it. Honest. I'll find it a home in just a few days."

Ruthann put her head to one side, considering. "Okay, I guess. Why do they have to die?"

" 'Cause nobody has adopted them yet, and Doc can't keep them any longer. They were just dumped there. Isn't that awful?"

"People are the pits," Ruthann agreed. "But my gramma isn't going to like this, so let's put him out in the barn. There's old straw for a bed, and I can give him milk and table scraps. But not for long, okay?"

Ruthann chose the smaller puppy, a female, and with Marty's help settled her in the barn. "Not too long, Marty, I mean it. I can't keep coming out here all the time. It's too suspicious, and it's a pain besides."

The next puppy placement went just as smoothly. Marty asked Mr. Timmons if he could talk to Rusty, and when Rusty came to the door, both of them walked down the Timmonses' sidewalk toward the backyard. Marty explained his problem as they walked. "So you can see how easy it'll be," he concluded. "Just a few days and I'll take him off your hands."

"You're sure?"

"Positive. You can keep him in your pool shed, with all the tools. Nobody'll go there now, in November. And if he makes any noise, he's too far away for your folks to hear. But maybe, to-night, you could feed him a little?"

Rusty said okay, and they settled the puppy on a pile of old rags in the pool shed. "How often does he eat?"

"Puppies like to eat three times a day, but just being alive is something for this one. Feed him as often as you can without getting caught." Marty pushed the empty puppy box into a corner of the shed. He felt as though a heavy load had been lifted from his shoulders. For now, all the puppies were safe. He had done it. At least for today.

Marty ran back to Holly Tree Court. *No point in worrying,* he told himself. He would find homes somehow. And Saturday he was going on the road with Hank. Now *that* was something to look forward to.

6.
On the Road

"Where to first?" Marty asked, settling next to Young Doc Number Two in the front seat of the station wagon.

"Carlson Farm, on the way to Chillicothe. Carlson wants us right now, too. Got a horse with a CUT FORELEG."

Hank's voice rose above the clanking of medicine bottles that rattled and joggled behind him in their wooden cases. A large stainless steel pail jiggled to and fro, adding its metallic music to the uproar. By the time they were up to highway speed, the din was overwhelming.

"Doesn't that stuff break sometimes?"

Hank leaned over toward Marty.

"I SAID, DOESN'T THAT STUFF BREAK?"
Hank smiled and shook his head no. "I
NEVER HEAR IT ANYMORE," he roared.
"LUCKY WE GOT A BEAUTIFUL DAY, ISN'T
IT?" He pursed his lips and began to whistle.

Marty could tell he was whistling only by how
he looked. The whistle itself was lost in the
racket made by the veterinary supplies. Marty
decided to whistle, too, because no one could
hear how awful his whistling was. He began
with "Happy Birthday," an easy one, and moved
on to the Ohio State Fight Song.

"HOW ABOUT 'JOHN JACOB JENKEL-
HEIMER SCHMIDT'?" Hank hollered compan-
ionably. Whistling together, or so they thought,
Marty and Hank clattered into the Carlson farm
and rolled to a stop at the barnyard gate.

Wade Carlson introduced himself and led
them to a stall in the barn. Marty peered over
the stall door and down at the horse's foreleg,
which oozed blood into the straw.

Hank let himself into the stall, and the
palomino danced around uneasily. She tossed
her head in the air and moved as far from the
stranger as possible.

"Whoa, Fairlight, easy now," soothed Mr.

Carlson. "She's not real friendly with everybody, Doc."

Hank stretched a hand toward Fairlight as if
to stroke her head and mane. Fairlight tried to
bite him and missed.

Hands in his pockets, Hank sighed. "You'll
have to hold her, Mr. Carlson, while I give her
a shot to calm her down. I'll never get a look at
the cut this way."

When Mr. Carlson stepped into the stall, Fair-
light rolled her eyes from one man to another.
Hank grinned. "I think she smells a plot, eh,
Marty?"

Hank filled a syringe with sedative, and Fairlight moved warily around her stall, growing
more and more upset. She threw her head and
mane in the air and whinnied. When she
brushed by the door of the stall, where Marty
watched, she snapped her teeth in his face.

"Holy crud!" Marty jumped back. "What's
with her?"

"She's a horse," Hank replied. "Horses and I
have this thing going. We don't get along."

Marty was taken aback. "I thought vets liked
all animals."

"Not if they're honest. Hold her still, Mr. Carlson, in the corner." He swiftly injected Fairlight with the sedative that would calm her and dull the pain of her wound.

Hank hopped out of the way as Fairlight's neck and head jerked around. "Nice horsie," he said as he slipped out of the stall. "We'll let that take effect, if you don't mind."

Mr. Carlson followed the vet out of the stall. "Don't like horses? Why'd they send you then? That Charlie Switzer, now *he* likes horses."

Hank leaned up against the roughness of the barn. "Yes, he's always liked big-animal work. So does Old Doc Cameron. Me, I'm a small-animal man. I'm a fool for a dog or a cat, even a rabbit. We balance well that way, but the vets have to divvy up the road calls, so here I am."

Mr. Carlson looked unconvinced. He glanced worriedly over the stall door. "Look at her now, Doc."

Fairlight stood with her head bowed, feet apart, eyes slightly dulled. *She looks asleep on her feet,* Marty thought.

Hank entered the stall and went to work. As he watched, Marty's full respect for Hank returned. First, the vet gave injections of local anaesthetic in a circle around the cut. He cleaned the wound thoroughly, talking to the horse and her owner all the time. "How'd she do this?" he asked as he probed the open gash. "It's deep and right in the joint. It's a bad one, Mr. Carlson."

Mr. Carlson said he hadn't a clue and watched morosely as Hank left the stall and went to the car for supplies.

"Here, Marty," Hank said on his return, "you hand this stuff to me when I ask for it."

With Marty's help, the treatment and sewing of Fairlight's wound went swiftly. In minutes, Hank was wrapping bandages around the joint of the leg and giving the horse a shot of antibiotic. "Has she had permanent tetanus shots?" he asked.

Mr. Carlson nodded.

"Good. Otherwise she'd need tetanus now. Have you ever given shots, by the way?"

Mr. Carlson said he had, so Hank left instructions, syringes, and antibiotic for Fairlight's continuing care. "Here're extra bandages. You'll have to remove the bandage, apply this salve, and redress that leg every day. Watch for redness or swelling or fever—any signs of infection—and don't forget the daily antibiotic shot.

One of us'll come back in three days, but call if there's a problem."

"Going to take six men and a boy to hold her," Mr. Carlson grumbled. "But I can't afford to have a vet come do it, not every day."

"I understand," replied Hank, smiling. "Come on, Marty. Next stop's a boarding stable. Lots of horsies. Lucky us!" He jumped into the front seat and off they went, bumping and clattering back onto the main road.

An elderly man named Mueller met them at the boarding stable. "If this is strangles, we got trouble," he said by way of introduction.

"What're strangles?" Marty asked. It sounded awful.

Mr. Mueller's answer was quick. "Not eating, sore throats, runny noses, sometimes coughing. Right, Doctor?"

Hank nodded soberly. "Short, but accurate. I think of it like mumps because there's often painful swelling under the jaws. Upper respiratory and very contagious, too."

Marty, who by now had admitted to himself that he wasn't fond of horses either, still felt sorry for any horse with strangles. He knew mumps would hurt, and was glad he'd been vaccinated against it long ago. "Can you cure it? They don't die, do they?"

Hank shook his head. "Hardly ever. Mr. Mueller runs a fine, clean stable and never overworks his horses. If they've got strangles, I'd say they picked them up at a show somewhere."

Mr. Mueller straightened with pride at Hank's compliment. "We try hard," he said briefly, "but I'm worried."

Hank examined the two horses that had caused Mr. Mueller so much worry. "Think we've just got a good case of flu here—influenza, to be precise," he said after a time. "I'll give them shots and expectorants for the coughing. Rest these horses—but then, I know you'd do that."

"Well," Mr. Mueller said heartily, "I am glad I called. Better to check than be sorry later, eh?"

Hank and Marty worked together to treat the horses, then packed their supplies and headed out. "Time for lunch," Hank told him as they got in the car.

For lunch, Hank chose a meadow and the shade of a late oak clinging stubbornly to its leaves. He pulled an old blanket from the rear of the wagon and spread it on the grass. From a cooler he offered Marty a can of pop. "Cream soda, Coke, or root beer?"

Marty chose the cream soda. He bit hungrily into his peanut butter and jelly sandwich, and they ate in silence. Then Hank stretched out on the blanket. "How about this for mid-November? I love southern Ohio. Blue sky. Big red leaves. Birds chirping at each other. Now this is a job, right?"

Marty stretched out and looked up at the oak, still aflame with color. "This's pretty good, all right. Even if you don't like horses."

"Yup. Can't have everything. If we were back at the hospital, I'd probably be talking on the phone with 'poor wuzzums'' mama about how the little dear is starving to death on his cruel diet." He chuckled.

"She calls a lot, huh?"

"All the time, but ol' Max will never starve with her around!" Hank yawned and stretched lazily. "We'll do cows this afternoon. Dairy farm check. Boring, but necessary."

"Do you always work on Saturdays?"

"Pretty near. I have one weekend off a month. Aren't enough of us to go around. Tomorrow I'll go into the hospital and check on the sick ones, and supervise the man who comes in to feed and clean the others on Sundays."

Working weekends was something else Marty hadn't thought about. "You must really like animals."

"Sure. And it beats vet school, even though I work more hours than I did in school. It's what I wanted to do, and now I'm doing it. It's more routine than I expected, but Old Doc is one heck of a vet—even if she does call me Baby Doc." He made a face.

"How . . ." Marty thought. "How did you know what you wanted to do? For *sure*, I mean?"

"I wasn't sure till I was halfway through vet med. Then I knew. Lots of people don't know until they do something for a while or change jobs a few times before they find the right one. My dad had five jobs before he settled in."

"I want to be a vet. At least most of the time I want to. Once, I was going to study bugs." Marty thought fondly of his bug collection, now defunct. He had saved all the jars and cages, though, just in case.

"Well, you don't have to decide today." Hank yawned again. "Let's split that last can of pop and get going before I fall asleep. We still have that dairy herd."

Marty helped as much as he could as they checked the herd. A routine check on cows was boring. This was a herd of Holsteins—big, big cows designed in black and white.

The feel of being in a barn with cows was different from the feeling Marty had had with Fairlight or at Mueller's stable. There he had felt the energy of the horses and their restlessness. Those barns had throbbed with horses.

Here with cows he felt how solid they were, how steady and quiet. The Holsteins munched their cuds and gazed at Marty with unquestioning eyes. Even their tails moved in a leisurely manner as they allowed the vet to examine them.

Hank called the farmer over to the side of a cow. "I've checked her and she's probably not going to calve again. She has a chronic enlargement of the uterus, which won't affect her health but will keep her from conceiving. I'm sorry if that's a problem."

"Doc, farming is problems. They're one and the same. When she runs dry, I'll sell her for beef."

Marty looked down to find several black-and-gray-striped kittens tumbling about his feet. A black mother cat arched her back and rubbed against his jeans.

"Take one of those kittens," the farmer told Marty. "Go on, boy, any one you like . . . or two or three!"

Marty shook his head violently. The farmer couldn't know his problem, he realized—and he had managed to forget it all day—but that was the *worst* idea Marty had heard in weeks. He already had three puppies to get rid of, for cripes' sake.

"Sorry, but my mom'd have a fit. I just took a guinea pig home a while ago, and we have a dog and three cats." *And three puppies,* the small voice in his head chimed.

"Tell your friends, then," the farmer insisted.

By four o'clock Hank was finally finished testing cows for pregnancy and giving vaccinations. He told the farmer his herd looked great, as he and Marty scrubbed cow manure off their boots and pant legs. Marty even found a wad of it on his jean jacket. A cow's tail must have flicked it there, he thought with disgust.

"GOOD DAY, RIGHT?" Hank yelled over the

clattering medicines, boxes, and metal pail as they headed home.

"GREAT DAY!" Marty roared back, the smell of cow manure filling his nostrils. He couldn't seem to like cow manure, especially when it was so close to his nose.

"KEPT EVERY SINGLE PATIENT. YOU NOTICED THAT?"

Marty grinned and nodded.

"SOME DAYS AREN'T SO HOT. SOME DAYS YOU LOSE AN ANIMAL." Hank stared ahead of him down the road. "BUT THAT'S THE WAY IT GOES." He shrugged philosophically.

Yes, Marty thought, *that's the way it goes.* He put the thought away from him. "HOW ABOUT SOME MORE 'JOHN JACOB JENKEL-HEIMER SCHMIDT'?" he suggested.

7.
A Case of Gok and Orphans

"Nine puppies?" Marty asked incredulously. "She had nine at once?" He thought of the kittens the farmer had tried to give him, and the three orphan puppies who were never far from his mind. The world was stuffed with kittens and puppies!

"Purebred Labrador retrievers," the owner replied proudly. "This's Juliet's second litter of nine."

Doc grinned at Marty and Tim over the basket of jet-black puppies. She had said, "Fine!" when Marty had asked if Tim could visit for an afternoon, and Tim was doing his best to be quiet and inconspicuous so that Marty didn't get into trouble.

"Marty, or Tim, somebody," Doc said, still smiling down at the puppies, "hand me that package of Magic Markers in the third drawer. We'll mark each puppy's ear a different color so we don't get mixed up and give some fellow two shots."

By the time Old Doc had marked a female puppy with chartreuse green, Marty and Tim were on the examining room floor, buried in seven puppies.

"After four or five," laughed Tim, "you hardly notice another one." He pulled a fat pup out from under the tail of his flannel shirt.

"Okay," Doc said, finishing the last puppy. "Let's have those stool samples now. I'd guess if one's got worms, they all have."

Turning to Marty, the dogs' owner said, "Under the front seat of our car. My daughter Susan is in the waiting room and can go out to the car with you to get the samples."

Marty found Susan reading a magazine. "Your mom wants us to get the stool samples from under the front seat of your car," he told her. A short time ago he'd have been embarrassed, but now he knew that stool samples were only routine.

Susan, who looked about sixteen, sucked in her breath. "Uh-oh. Have we got a problem." She stood up and led the way down the hall to Doc's room.

"Mom," Susan said, "Kenny brought us Dad's car. He said you'd promised he could take *your* car on his date with that new girl he keeps talking about. He took the car we came in."

"And the stool samples," added Mrs. Robertson.

"He took her for a *drive*," Susan said, her mouth twitching at the corners.

Marty and Tim looked at each other, both keeping their laughter inside.

But Old Doc chuckled out loud. "Lucky, lucky boy," she murmured. "Bring the samples in later then. Let's check Juliet now before you leave."

Marty, Tim, and Susan wallowed amid puppies on the floor while Old Doc went over Juliet. After some time Doc said, "You've got me. I don't know what ails her. Another case of gok."

"She's said that before," Marty whispered to Tim. Louder, he asked, "Doc, what is that gok stuff?"

Doc turned from the Labrador to Marty and

Tim. "God only knows," she said. "I don't."

"God only knows," repeated Marty. "Gok. Can we cure it?"

Doc smiled. "Usually. Right now, Juliet's running a low temperature and doesn't seem very sick. Looks good for a new mother, in fact. But we always feel we have to *do* something, even though this injection I'm giving her may not be exactly the right thing." She shook her head. "The more we learn, the fewer cases of gok we'll see." She lowered the examining table to the floor. Juliet was immediately engulfed in puppies.

"Sort of a vacation for her up on my table. She'd probably like to come back tomorrow for another rest." Doc stroked the Lab's shiny black coat. "She looks fine. Must be a mild case of gok. But bring her right in if she doesn't eat, seems restless, or unduly tired. You know the symptoms," she said to Mrs. Robertson.

When the Robertsons and their dogs had been packed into their car, Old Doc told Marty and Tim to help with cage cleaning. "You're a good worker, Marty," she said as she bent over to pull on her farm boots. "Hope you're enjoying it here."

"Oh, he is," Tim said loyally. Then he looked

embarrassed, as if he thought he shouldn't have said anything.

"It's great, Doc." Marty paused. "But . . . but I'm still mad about those cats. You know, the ones whose owners forgot them?"

Old Doc shook her head. "No they didn't. Remember, I told you one's out of the country. Another's moving. It's not cheap to board an animal, Marty, and those owners will come and get their pets as soon as they can. Well, I'm off." She stood up, stomped her boots, and left Marty and Tim to clean dog cages with John.

Marty told himself that he really was enjoying his job as he slopped a mop inside a cage. Of course, nobody liked cleaning cages much. But most of the work was fine.

Farther down the row of cages, Tim and John also worked. John squeezed soapy disinfectant out of his mop and said he wasn't sure he was going to finish a term paper due before Thanksgiving vacation.

"Yeah," Marty agreed. "They give way too much homework." Privately, he told himself one more time to hurry up and get organized. And then there were the puppies to worry about.

"Jason took one of those puppies," he told Tim and John.

"Good for him," Tim said. "Wish I could've."

"You were just lucky," John insisted. "How about the others?"

"I've got some ideas," Marty replied quickly. That wasn't true, but Marty's pride was strong.

"Doc says people should come looking for pets. Then you can figure they'll make good homes. Talking people into it is no good." John stuck his mop down into the disinfectant and went outside to the dog runs.

Gloomily, Marty nodded. "You know, Tim, Ruthann and Rusty are great sitters, but I think they're getting nervous because I haven't got real homes yet."

"Call them tonight and say it'll be any minute," Tim suggested. "You'll have homes any day now."

Any day now, Marty thought, as he ran fresh water into bowls. His trouble was that he had almost no time. School, work, supper, bed. Every day the same. He and Tim were both expected to help around the house for part of each weekend, so their times together were fewer than they had hoped. Meanwhile, time went flying by.

On the telephone that night, both Rusty and Ruthann were firm. "A couple more days, Marty," Ruthann said. "I mean it. I'm telling

Gramma I run around the yard for exercise, but she thinks I'm crazy, and she's suspicious every time I go outdoors to feed that puppy!"

Marty promised her immediate action and he promised Rusty the same thing.

In bed, Marty stewed about the orphan puppies, alone and lonely in the barn at Ruthann's and the shed at Rusty's house. No mother dog, no father dog, no family of any kind. He couldn't imagine life without his family. Of course, there were kids who didn't have families, just like the puppies.

"That's it!" he said aloud.

"Go to sleep, Marty. You're hopping and flopping around up there, and I'm never going to get to sleep." Jut yawned, and Marty could hear him punching his pillow into position.

"I got it!" Marty leaned over the edge of his bunk. "I'll bet the orphans' home will take these puppies for their kids. It'd be great for them. Very good psychology and I'll tell 'em that, too," Marty concluded happily.

"Mmm-hmm," Jut agreed. "Go to sleep."

The next day in school was not one of Marty's finest. He got back three English papers, two B minuses and a C. He had never liked B's or C's much, no matter what anyone said about those being good or average grades. He didn't mind plain old B's. They were okay, although he preferred A's. But C's he hated. He told himself that he had been cheated, that the papers deserved higher grades. After looking them over, he decided, sadly, that the grades were fair after all.

If I don't watch it, he thought, *I'll get blasted on mid-quarter slips or my report card in January. Mom'll have a fit.* Mad clear through, Marty wadded each of the unhappy papers into a ball and marched them to the wastepaper basket beside Mrs. Albert's desk.

"Something wrong, Marty?" Mrs. Albert kept her voice low so as not to disturb the quiet working period.

"It's my own fault." Marty turned to go back to his seat.

"Wait, Marty. Didn't Tim tell me you were working after school at Doc Cameron's?"

He nodded. "I can do better. I just haven't given homework enough time."

"This is a difficult year, and I'm a tough grader." She softened the words with a smile. "You're a fine student, and you can bring those grades up."

Grateful, Marty smiled back. "Starting now," he promised. He made himself concentrate fiercely all day long, pushing thoughts of the orphan puppies out of his mind.

With the hum of the three-fifteen buzzer in his ears, Marty's mind went right back to the puppies. As he piled books into his locker, he decided to take the puppies with him to the orphanage. What Jut had said was true. It was much harder to reject a live puppy. *I ought to know*, he thought.

Hoping not to be very late for work, Marty hurried to collect the puppies. When he reached the orphanage, he asked to speak to the director. The receptionist wanted to know why.

Marty fixed her with his most pleading look. "It's urgent business. He'll want to see me when he knows what it is."

The receptionist hesitated, then buzzed the director. "There's a boy to see you, Dr. Dinsmore. He says it's urgent business." She listened to her earphones. "Yes, sir.

"You're to wait here a few minutes. Then he'll see you."

"That's wonderful." Marty sat down on a tired, brown, leather-looking sofa. He held the box on his lap and prayed that the puppies wouldn't start yapping. He felt his glasses way at the end of his nose, where they looked weird and felt weirder. He was sick of their not staying in place like most other people's glasses did.

From inside the box came an unhappy whimper. And another. Marty started to whistle as camouflage. The box jiggled on his lap and he held it tighter. "John Jacob Jenkelheimer Schmidt . . ." whistled Marty. Mentally he rehearsed what he was going to say to the director.

A tall, slim man poked his head around the office door. "Did you want to see me?" he asked Marty.

Marty jumped to his feet. "Yessir. Thank you very much, sir. Could we go into your office?"

The director held the door open for Marty and his box. "What can I do for you? I'm Dr. Dinsmore." He held out his hand.

Marty set the box down and shook hands. "Martin Howard, Dr. Dinsmore, and I have something very special for your orphanage."

The director smiled politely and sat down behind his desk. "You do? Well, if it costs any money, Mr. Howard, you'll have to take it elsewhere. This orphanage operates on the world's shortest shoestring."

"That's just what I was thinking. No money for extras—and plenty of needy kids. Especially needing love and affection." Marty could tell he had the director's complete attention, so he raced on.

"Love and affection are more important than food or clothes. More important than anything, right?"

Looking dazed, Dr. Dinsmore nodded.

"Well, I have some absolutely free love and affection right here in this box. What I have needs these orphans just as much as they need it—ah, them."

He opened the box and held up the two furry puppies. "Giving these little dogs love won't cost anything. But think what the kids will get in return. It's the most *psychological thing* you could do for this whole place."

Dr. Dinsmore blinked.

Marty hammered away. "I saw a program on TV about kids with problems. *They gave them each a pet.* It was very good psychology, because those kids got better *after* they got the pet."

Sitting very straight in his chair, Dr. Dinsmore nodded as Marty spoke. "I see. And did this program say who paid for the food for these wonderful pets?"

"No, but don't your kids leave little bits of stuff on their plates, like peas or lima beans, or maybe meat that's tough? Dogs *love* those things, and it's good for them, too. Perfect balanced diet, just from leftovers."

Marty remembered Lucky, Wheatstraw, Major, and Princess. "The more vegetables they get, the less doggy odor they're going to have ... I think. And you'll use hardly any garbage bags because there won't be any garbage left over, thanks to these good pets. And kids won't get sick so much either, because they'll be *happier*, and my friend Miss Brown, who's a nurse, says happy people are healthier."

Dr. Dinsmore stood up. "Stop, Martin. I believe you." He reached across the desk to pet both puppies. "I feel like I've been sold, but you did such a good job of it that I don't mind. You know, I saw that same TV program, and I was thinking about getting a dog or cat and giving it a try. I honestly was. But I hadn't thought of *two*."

Exultant, Marty hugged both puppies to his chest. "You wouldn't separate a brother and a sister, would you? You don't do that here, do you?"

Dr. Dinsmore sat back down again. "You hit me where I live. Tell me that you don't sell anything else, Martin, because I can't take any more." Then he smiled, not just politely this time.

Marty sagged with relief. "They were going to die," he told Dr. Dinsmore. "But I saved them. It wasn't right. I knew it wasn't right to take them to the pound, even if John said there would be more."

"Sit down, Martin. Just let the puppies run around a minute. Who's John? And more of what?"

Marty put the puppies down and sat in the chair across from the director's desk. He told about his job then: about John, and cleaning dog cages, and the cats that had been at Old Doc's for so long, about how he hardly ever saw his best friend because of his job. He explained how a mother cat had lost all her kittens that just wouldn't be born, and how people left perfectly good animals at the vets' hospital to be put to sleep, or, if lucky, to be adopted. He couldn't remember when he had just blabbed on this way.

Dr. Dinsmore listened and nodded. Now and then he said, "Mmm, terrible," in agreement with Marty. When Marty was finished, Dr. Dins-

91

more said, "Your work sounds much like mine, and I've always thought that what I did was important. Maybe important jobs have problems to match, what do you think?"

"I think yes," Marty replied.

After their talk Dr. Dinsmore and Marty took the puppies, left the office, and went toward a gym next to the main building. On the way, they met a teenaged girl who had two little girls by the hands.

When the girls found out that Hampshire Orphanage was now the owner of the puppies, each was ready to play mother. From the amount of hugging and petting that went on, Marty could see that the puppies had come home. He had been right to save them, because they belonged here.

"Feels good?" Dr. Dinsmore asked Marty.

"It sure does." Marty stood still and let himself feel good all over. And then, though he didn't want to leave, he said good-bye before he was any later for work.

Dr. Dinsmore held out his hand for the second time. "I enjoyed meeting you. If you get tired of the vets' place, Marty, you might try being a salesman sometime."

Marty jogged all the way to work. He had a little nagging doubt that jogged with him, however. The doubt said he had talked Dr. Dinsmore into these puppies—just the thing Old Doc and John felt was wrong. But then he thought of Dr. Dinsmore, how nice he was, how understanding, and how he had been ready to get a pet for the orphanage anyway. It was a matter of knowing *how* to talk somebody into something, he decided, and *who*. His dad sold computers. *He must have passed along some of that selling talent to me,* Marty thought happily.

8.
A Surprise in the Waiting Room

When Thanksgiving Thursday and its long weekend arrived, Marty was ready for a break. He promised Old Doc he would help John on Friday, to shorten John's time at work, but on Thanksgiving Day itself and Saturday and Sunday, Marty was wonderfully free. He ate hot turkey, cold turkey sandwiches, and turkey under gravy on toast. He and Tim spent one night together at the Howards' house, and one at Tim's house, where they watched an old late-night Western on TV. He forgot about homework altogether in his enjoyment, and he didn't even have to worry about orphans.

On the last night, Sunday, Jut yawned across

his desk at Marty. "Here we go again. I have spent my whole sophomore year with my face in this world history book."

Happily, Marty yawned back at him. "Yeah, but it was a great weekend. You should have seen those kids' faces when they knew the puppies were staying at the orphanage," he said, for perhaps the fifth time in as many days.

"I am talking about *work*," Jut said grumpily.

"So am I!" Marty retorted. "I work more'n you do. And I'll be blind by Christmas from all this reading for English!"

Marty and Jut argued about who was busiest until the subject was exhausted and Jut left the room to take his shower. Marty went back to his book, except that he thought about the great Christmas presents he'd be able to buy this year with the pot of money he was earning at Doc's hospital.

Marty tried to concentrate on homework because Christmas always made him think about being extra good—or extra responsible. He had heard the song "Santa Claus Is Coming to Town" when he was Gus's age. He couldn't explain why, but he had believed every word of it, especially the part where it said that Santa saw you when you were sleeping and knew when you were awake. He wasn't sure that was fair. Only God was supposed to know what you did every minute. If he thought about it, Marty could imagine a host of seen and unseen beings watching every move he made.

Marty forced himself back to his book. He needed to bring up his grades, for himself—not for Santa, not even for God. He wanted to keep his job. Even if he'd had some trouble placing the puppies, it had been worth it. He hadn't had nearly as much trouble as everyone thought he would. It had been easy, in fact. A cinch.

The next afternoon at work Marty was overjoyed to learn that Saber's owner had come for her over the weekend. He would miss her, but she had never really liked him. *She just tolerated me,* he realized, *and waited.*

Boots, youngest of the boarders, was also gone. "She was supposed to be a little girl's pet," Vicki told him, "only the kid got awfully sick, so we got Boots. Now the kid's well, and Boots isn't much of a kitten anymore, but he's gone home."

Now only Gretchen, the calico, and Samson, the male, were left of the cats he had worried so much about. Probably they, too, would go home before long. Old Doc was right again, Marty decided, somewhat reluctantly. *Don't worry unless worry is needed.* He told Vicki he was going to play with Gretchen and Samson for a while before he got too busy. Maybe he could learn not to worry, but he still cared about them.

Later, as they cleaned cages, Marty asked John, "Are they all on the road? I haven't seen anybody."

"Baby Doc and Doc are, yeah, but Charlie said you could help him if you want. Come back, though. Old Doc called in, and she wants us to mop the waiting-room floor before we leave."

Marty promised to help John later, and went down the hall to Dr. Switzer's examining room. He hadn't worked with him yet. It felt good to know that Dr. Switzer wanted him.

As he came through the door he heard the vet's voice raised in anger. "You see this?"

Marty peered around Dr. Switzer's back to see what was causing the fuss. The vet was holding up the paw of a standard poodle. It was dirty and oozing blood, and the dog was whimpering.

"This animal's in a lot of pain and going to have a lot more before he's through." Dr.

Switzer's anger was directed at two teenagers who had backed against the wall of the room.

"Idiots who throw bottles out of car windows ought to be forced to walk on the broken glass just like this dog has!"

The boy and girl nodded. Marty looked at Dr. Switzer's face and thought he'd never seen anyone so mad.

"Year after year, people who don't give a damn about anyone or anything else cause animals—and people—a lot of grief from broken glass. It's just plain stupid to throw anything out of a car window!" He reached for the disinfectant bottle. "I'll have to try to dig for the bits of glass embedded in this dog's paws."

The teenagers, frozen against the wall, didn't make a sound. Marty pushed his glasses up on his nose and didn't say anything either. He hadn't seen any of the vets behave like this before, but he understood. It was how he had felt when he took Gooney Pig home—whenever he saw the long-term boarders in their cages—when he had vowed to find homes for the three puppies.

"Marty, you hold the back end of this poodle while I give him a shot. Otherwise, he'll never sit still for this probing."

Marty looked at the teenagers and thought that the girl was going to cry. He was pretty sure the dog wouldn't feel anything. The vets never caused pain if they could help it. But the girl and boy didn't know that. Suddenly Marty was sure that part of Dr. Switzer's behavior was an act. He was carrying on like this on purpose.

Burying a smile in the thick curls on the poodle's back, Marty held on while the vet anaesthetized the dog's front paws. The big poodle didn't like the shots and tried to pull away. "What's his name?" Marty asked in the awkward silence.

"Noah Webster," the boy answered woodenly. "We just call him Noah, and we, uh, we wouldn't ever throw bottles out of a car, would we, Sara?"

Sara shook her head back and forth.

"Good," Dr. Switzer said. "Tell your friends about it. Maybe they won't either." He began to make careful slits in the pads of Noah's left forepaw. "I have to follow where I think the glass has gone to see if I find glass splinters."

"I think I'm going to barf," Sara said.

"Take her to the waiting room," Dr. Switzer told the boy. "This isn't pretty work. Sorry." Dr.

Switzer's intense blue eyes and normally smiling mouth were grim as he spoke.

Both teenagers left the office, and Marty moved to where he could see better.

"This doesn't bother you?" the vet asked as he worked on the dog's footpads. Blood was flowing freely out of the fresh cuts, and Marty hoped that glass splinters were being washed out, too.

"I feel sorry for Noah, but he doesn't feel anything now, does he? Wouldn't he be yipping or something?" Marty petted the poodle, who was watching his operation with curiosity.

"Without the anaesthetic we couldn't work on him. But I get so cussed mad every time I have to get a dog out of this fix that I have to say something!" His eyes were blue ice.

"You get mad very good."

"Thank you. I meant every word of it. When the feeling returns to these paws, this poodle's going to hurt. If I can convince even ten people to stop heaving trash out their car windows, I'll be satisfied." He reached for paper towels.

"Marty, you keep wiping up. We'll give him a shot of antibiotic when we think we've got all the glass out, and maybe he won't get an infection."

When Noah had two bandaged paws and his shot, Marty and Dr. Switzer took him out to the waiting room.

"Your instructions are on this sheet of paper, and here are pills he must take to prevent infection. I want to see him again in three days."

Sara and her boyfriend promised to bring Noah back. "Thanks a lot. We wouldn't ever throw bottles out of a car. I'm not kidding," said the boy as he went out the door.

"On that note," Dr. Switzer told Marty, "I'm going home. Tell John to lock up as usual." Smile back in place, he reached for his coat.

As Marty helped John mop the waiting room later, he told him about Dr. Switzer and the broken glass in Noah's paws.

"It's his crusade," John said. "That and barbed-wire fences. Hates broken glass and barbed-wire fences something awful. So do Baby Doc and Doc. All three of 'em just give people hell on those subjects. Stick around and you'll hear Old Doc one of these days. She scares 'em to death."

"What's this box for?" Marty pushed his mop against a large cardboard box in the corner of

the waiting room. The box was nearly hidden by a leafy fern.

"You got me. I've never seen it before." John looked across the room.

With the bump of Marty's mop, the box began mewing and scratching as it jostled itself on the smooth tile floor. Marty knew before he opened it what he would see. When he pulled the box top free of the tape someone had used to close the box, there they were. Kittens. Six very young kittens. Left in the vets' waiting room.

Marty stared down at them, then out the broad picture window at the parking lot. The window showed every inch of the parking lot and not one car was there. This box was no mistake. It had been left behind on purpose.

"Crum!" John had dragged his mop over to where Marty knelt by the box. "These guys are hardly old enough to leave their mother!"

"Does this happen a lot?"

"I told you. There's always more. I told you that."

Marty's shoulders sagged. Moved by a mixture of pity for the kittens and rage at whoever had left them, he put his hand in the box. The kittens tumbled around Marty's hand, licking and chewing with sharp, hungry teeth.

"Why do they leave them *here*? Why don't they take them to the pound?"

"Nobody likes to do that. They think we'll take care of them or find them homes, maybe. How do I know? Only Doc's sick of it, and we've placed so many this fall already. . . ."

"What'll we *do*?"

"Put 'em in a cage on Pussycat Lane, with food, for now. Tomorrow, Doc'll probably tell us to take 'em to the pound. I can't think what else. Nobody'll want them."

Nobody will want them. The past month at the vets' hospital whirled in Marty's mind. There had been good things, of course. Many animals were well that had been sick—dozens of happy stories. But it was the unhappy stories that burned in his memory. Animals got a raw deal, Marty thought. It just wasn't fair.

"I'll take them," he said.

"I've heard that before. Look, Marty, you can't take—"

"Yes I can," Marty interrupted. *Of course I can. Didn't I find a home for Gooney Pig? And the three orphan puppies? It was easy. If you're determined—and if you're a salesman—you can do it. I can do it again.*

When the waiting room was cleaned, Marty and John locked up and left. John hopped on his bike and waved good-bye. Marty walked toward home, with another box in his arms.

9.
A Small Shazzam

The kittens mewed hungrily and racketed around inside their box as Marty trudged homeward. He held the box close to his chest and wondered what he was going to do this time.

His mother had been okay about letting Gooney Pig move into their family. She always let Nick bring home the white mice from school to spend the weekend. Even Gus had once brought home the nursery-school parrot for a visit.

But she was firm about not adopting any more strays. "Gooney is absolutely it," she had said. "Our zoo is complete."

So what on earth was he going to do with these

106

kittens? Nick had opened his big mouth and bragged about how the three puppies had been placed—one by him, personally, at Jason's house—and they had had to confess about the puppies. "You were mighty lucky," Mrs. Howard had told Marty. "Better not press your luck. You know what I said about no more pets."

But here he was, with another box full of animals that nobody wanted. If only it were morning and he had all day . . . Instead it was dark, nearly suppertime, and his hands were freezing. Marty had several mittens, no two alike, but they were in his locker at school. Could he keep the kittens in his locker and give them away at lunch and after school?

"Dumb, dumb, dumb," Marty said out loud. If he tried to hide them in his and Jut's closet, his parents might find out. He had been awfully nervous when the puppies were in the closet. No, not that again.

He needed time—time to ask around and see who wanted a kitten. It was only three weeks till Christmas. Maybe he could convince people what great Christmas gifts they'd make. Marty walked faster.

The people who had baby-sat with the puppies

probably wouldn't want to do it again, Marty reasoned. For the kittens, he needed somebody fresh. And if somebody just kept them in a basement or someplace, *he* could come to feed and water them. They'd be no trouble that way.

"Mrs. Thomas!" Marty stopped abruptly. "Mrs. Thomas," he said to the box of kittens, "is your new mother. Betcha anything. It's just for a few days."

Mrs. Thomas lived around the corner from the Howards on Grove Street. The Howards' backyard joined Mrs. Thomas's backyard. Her husband had died, her only daughter married and moved, and she was lonely. When Marty's mother had been home sick a couple years ago, Mrs. Thomas had kept Gus every day for weeks. She loved children, but more important to Marty, she also loved animals.

Still, Mrs. Thomas wasn't sure about mothering six kittens. "You say somebody just *left* them in the waiting room?" she asked Marty for the second time.

Marty nodded, understanding how she felt. "They leave animals all the time, like I said." He told her about the three orphan puppies. "So if the kittens could just stay on your back porch for a few days, I'll find them homes. They'd make great Christmas presents!"

"If I didn't have Mitzi and her oldest kitten, I'd take one myself, Marty, but I just can't. It costs so much to feed them, and now that Mr. Thomas's gone . . ." Her voice trailed off.

"How about if I come over twice a day? I'll bring their food and feed them myself. I'll change the water, put out clean kitty litter—do the whole thing."

"They'd be safe on the porch. It's all closed in. But if there's a problem, Marty, you'll have to take them somewhere else." She tried to look stern.

Marty smiled comfortably at her because he knew she couldn't be stern. "I promise. No problems. I'll put 'em on the porch and be right back with their stuff."

At home, in his garage, Marty stealthily loaded up what he needed for the kittens. He took an unopened sack of dry cat food, a low plastic plant pot that could hold water, and a cardboard box for kitty litter. He put all of these supplies, plus kitty litter, in one of the sacks his mother kept for garbage. Then he fixed up everything on Mrs. Thomas's porch. The kittens could sleep in their box where they'd be warm, all huddled together, even if it got cold. As he left, the kittens were nudging each other to get at the food Mrs. Thomas had put out for them in an old pie pan.

"You don't need to help," he said.

"I'll just get them started." Mrs. Thomas winked at him.

Marty slid into his chair at the supper table as the family was beginning their dessert, rainbow sherbet, a favorite of his. "Sorry," he mumbled, knowing that his mother liked to serve a meal once and be done with it.

Tonight, however, his mother was more concerned than angry. "Marty, isn't this job running into more hours than you figured?"

"You work more than I do," Mr. Howard added, before Marty had a chance to answer.

Mrs. Howard pressed on. "Is it worth it, son? I know you've still got homework." She nodded at the pile of books he'd dropped by the kitchen door on his way in.

"Well," Marty managed through a mouthful of meatloaf, "I really *like* it at Old Doc's." He chewed reflectively, thinking of the homework still ahead. "But I have to write a book report *and* a speech for Careers Week."

Jut licked his last spoonful of sherbet and stood up. "Yeah, but at least you've got a career to talk about. I remember Careers Week, and it was a pain. How's a guy supposed to know what he wants to do in seventh grade?"

"It's only meant to be an opportunity to explore a field that you find interesting. Shouldn't be too difficult for you now, Marty. Tell them some of the things that you've done and seen, firsthand." His father smiled encouragingly. "Should be the best talk in the class."

"Absolutely," Marty's mother added.

Marty sat up straighter. "Sure," he agreed, brightening. "I can tell about people leaving animals at the vets' all the time, just because they don't want 'em anymore, and how the vets work nearly every weekend. . . ." He stopped to help himself to carrots. He loathed cooked carrots, but they were the route to rainbow sherbet.

"That wouldn't sell *me* on bein' a vet," Nick announced loudly.

"Does sound a little depressing," Mr. Howard admitted. "Aren't there any good stories in your repertoire?"

111

"Of course," Marty replied quickly. He went on to tell about Juliet and her nine jet-black puppies, about the deaf white kitten who had two old men to care for him, and the marvelous speed with which Old Doc had neutered Hannibal Green.

Gus clanked his spoon on the table. "I wanta play Chutes and Ladders, Marty. You never play with me anymore." For a small chin, Gus's looked extremely stubborn.

Marty looked away from him and caught sight of his homework. "See, Gus? I have to do homework." He felt guilty, though, and sorry for Gus, who was happiest when Marty played with him. "Christmas vacation. I promise."

"That's not till forever," Gus grumbled, getting down from his chair.

As Gus wandered away from the table, Marty attacked his rainbow sherbet. He wasn't wild about Chutes and Ladders, but it was better than writing a speech and a book report. If he hadn't been at work all afternoon, those papers would be finished by now, and he could entertain Gus. Or watch TV. He for sure wouldn't be thinking about six homeless kittens. "Don't suppose I could have any more sherbet?" he asked.

Mrs. Howard shook her head. "You're eating a lot these days, Marty. Must be a growth spurt. More meatloaf or potatoes or carrots? How about an apple?"

Sighing, Marty took the apple and rubbed it on his jeans to clean it. "Got to start that book report. You know, Mom, that *ruins* the book. I keep trying to tell Mrs. Albert that, and she doesn't understand."

"I saw Mrs. Albert in the grocery store today, after school, and she says your grades are slipping. I can see that you love working with the vets, but you know our agreement. . . ." She let the rest of her words go unsaid.

"I know, I know. She grades hard, though." *I should have said that earlier in the year,* Marty thought, *so they'd be prepared.*

"Junior high is harder," his mother agreed. She poured herself a cup of coffee. "And we can all see that you're trying. We just don't want you under too much pressure, okay?" She picked up her book and left the kitchen, while Marty ran water in his sherbet dish before he put it into the dishwasher. Now he had to go upstairs, write a speech, write a book report, shower, and go to bed. Big deal. Just like every day. He hoped God and Santa Claus were watching, because he sure was being good.

"All teachers really want," Jut told Marty later as he labored over the book report, "is *analysis*. They already know the story, so make that part short. Then tell what's good about the book and what's lousy, and say whether you recommend it or not. That's all there is to it. You always make a big deal out of it, Marty."

Marty chewed the end of his pen. "Reading the book is fine," he insisted. "It's this writing part that stinks."

"You just haven't done it enough. It gets easier. Much easier than world history. This stuff goes on forever." Jut closed his book impatiently.

"Make you a deal. I'll quiz you on world history, and you write my book reports." Marty smiled his big, fake-funny smile.

"Very funny, Marty. Why'd you wait until tonight, anyway?"

"I've been busy!" Marty snapped. "In case you forgot, *I* have a job." He paused. "And you know what else I've got?"

Jut made a face. "I bet I don't want to know."

"Six kittens. Real little ones. Left in the waiting room today. Do you believe that?"

Jut shook his head. "What'd they think would happen to them?"

"I don't think they care. But John says the hospital can't get rid of any more, so I took 'em to Mrs. Thomas."

"What if she tells Mom? Is she going to keep them?"

"She promised not to tell, but she can't keep any. She'll just baby-sit until I find homes for them. Too bad everybody we know got one of Eleanore's kittens."

Jut let his breath out in a long whistle. "Hope your salary's worth all this. What're you going to do if you can't find homes? We don't live in New York, you know. This is little ol' Hampshire, population ten thou tops."

Marty knew what he meant. Hampshire was a small town by most people's standards. Still, in their area of Ohio, they were a "big town" where people came to shop and buy groceries. All the smaller towns around took the *Hampshire Weekly Gazette* as their paper.

That was it! Advertise the kittens in the *Gazette*. Rusty Timmons's mother worked for the paper, and that's where Rusty had advertised his summer job service and made millions.

"No sweat," he told Jut. "I'll advertise free kittens in the *Gazette* and that'll be that. Shazzam! No kittens."

"If you say so." Jut shucked off his sweatshirt and yawned his way to the shower.

Feeling better than he had in several hours, Marty settled down and wrote his report the way Jut had suggested. It wasn't bad, he thought, reading it over. Better than others he had done. He added two commas where they looked good, signed his name at the bottom, and put the report in his notebook. He needed an A on this paper because his English grades were teetering in B minus territory, and that meant trouble with his mother.

That night, before he went to sleep, Marty made time to play with Eleanore and Pierpont and the kittens, Fishhead and Licky. They played a game called Hide in the Bag, which Marty had invented long ago. He put brown grocery sacks, opened widely at one end, around their kitchen floor. Eleanore and her kittens, who were grown up now, crept into the bags. Pierpont went from one bag to another, snuffling and gurgling in his throat. After he had snorkeled at one cat's sack a few times, that cat zipped out past his slow-moving form and traded sacks with another cat. It was fast and funny and all of them knew it was a game.

"Isn't it your bedtime?" Mrs. Howard asked on her way through the kitchen.

"Just hadn't done this in a long time," Marty said apologetically. Time, he decided as he put away the grocery sacks, was certainly shorter than it used to be.

10.
Euthanasia, A Tough Word

Marty's next few days were busier than ever. He left for school early every morning so that he could feed the kittens, and raced to the grocery store after school to buy cat food and kitty litter to replace what he'd taken out of the garage.

He was appalled at the price of these items. Just for the first week's food, he figured he had had to work three hours. The kitty litter was worth two more hours of work, and it wouldn't last any time at all. The ad in the *Gazette* would run for three Wednesdays, but it had cost $5.50. Of course, all the kittens would be gone in three weeks—in new homes.

When he added it up, Marty's first week of kitten expenses came to $15.50. Taking care of the kittens could make a noticeable hole in the fat Christmas pot he'd been building to buy extra-special presents. He had had no time to shop, and now he was almost afraid to. He didn't know how much he might have to spend to support the kittens until they were adopted.

With these dismal thoughts, Marty stomped into work on a gray, cloudy December Saturday. He had gotten up much earlier than normal so that he could work a long day and earn more. He couldn't remember thinking about money before. Somehow, since he'd started earning money, it was on his mind often.

Marty started to clean dog cages. He told himself it was silly to worry about the kittens. The ad had already brought two calls to Mrs. Thomas that she had told him about. Both callers, she had said, had wanted fancy cats, with long fur or of a special breed. Marty's cats were tiger-striped or gray, with markings in white, and they were short-haired. Not fancy at all. Nonetheless, two calls had to mean something.

When he finished cleaning cages, Marty went to Old Doc's examining room to see if he could help with morning patients. Saturday was always a busy day.

The patient already in Doc's room was an elderly setter named Dog. His full name was Dog Grayson and he did not look well.

"I think it's time," Old Doc was saying as Marty peered around her to get a better look. "He's past the point where we can do anything for him. You said he's not eating and he's sleeping all the time. The tests show his kidney function is very badly impaired. And he can't see. I'm afraid . . ." Her hand stroked the thin, stubbly fur on the setter's back.

Mrs. Grayson nodded. "I warned my family when we left that this might be the end. I know you've done all you could." She, too, petted Dog as she spoke. "Best put him to sleep then." She bent over and kissed Dog's head, and Marty could see the tears in her eyes. "You've been a good boy, Dog. Dad and I'll miss you." Her tears dropped on Dog's head. "Do it quickly, please. I hate to blubber in public."

"He won't feel anything," Doc said as she prepared an injection. "All sensation is gone in only thirty seconds. Euthanasia is much kinder than letting them spend their final days in pain. It's the last thing we do for them, but sometimes it is the best." She pulled Dog's forepaw toward her and gave him the shot. Dog lay still, as he had all along, and Marty could see no difference in the stillness.

Old Doc put her hand over Mrs. Grayson's where it rested on Dog's head. "You are so good with animals, you and Mr. Grayson, that you ought to get another. After a time, of course."

Mrs. Grayson wiped her eyes. "After a bit. Here, let's put him in his box. I'll bury him out back with our cat. They were good friends."

Marty saw how tenderly Mrs. Grayson put her pet into the box. He couldn't think of a single helpful thing to say or do. Old Doc had helped, but he couldn't seem to.

"Hold the doors for Mrs. Grayson, Marty, and go on out to her car with her," Doc told him.

When Marty shut the car door behind Dog, he turned to Mrs. Grayson. "I bet he had a good life."

"He was part of our family." She put the car into reverse and backed away, and Marty waved until he could no longer see the car.

Inside, he joined Old Doc just in time to hear her embark on her new-puppy speech. It was the speech she gave to everyone who brought in a new puppy. This time she turned to Marty. "Why don't you give this talk?" Her eyes danced behind the glasses. "You must have it memorized by now."

Marty swallowed, looked at the young couple who stood by the table, then at the puppy. The puppy's pink tongue lolled out of his mouth. He was fat and furry and frisky—everything a puppy ought to be. "He looks just right," Marty said, embarrassed to be asked to give the speech. "Uh, did Doc tell you about feeding?"

"Not yet," the woman said, "just about the three rounds of puppy shots. What are they for besides distemper?"

Without thinking, Marty said, "Puppy shots protect against canine distemper, canine hepatitis, two kinds of leptospirosis, kennel cough, and parvo virus."

Everyone laughed as they realized that Marty must have parroted Doc word for word. "I guess I can give this speech," he said, relaxing. "It's important to have all three rounds of these shots, okay?"

Marty explained how a new puppy should be underfed at first until it gets used to its new home. He warned against offering much milk because it could give the puppy diarrhea. He cautioned them about other things, like rich foods, that would also create diarrhea, and he wasn't embarrassed at all. He gave them their free bottle of vitamin and mineral supplements, told them to check the stools for signs of worms, and recommended lots of brushing instead of baths. He talked about fleas, ticks, and ear mites.

"Well, I never did it better," Old Doc said when he finally finished. "That ought to have answered your questions and then some." She winked at Marty. "Man, can you talk."

"Did I say too much?" Marty smoothed the downy fur on the puppy's back—so different from the stiff, elderly stubble of Dog Grayson.

"No, sir," Doc assured him. "I have retired from the new-puppy field. After I examine a puppy and give the shot, *you* take over."

Marty basked in her approval, because he knew she wasn't just trying to make him feel good. He had done well. And it was sure better than helping put an animal to sleep. Euthanasia, as Old Doc called it, was a tough word.

But euthanasia became the word of the day, its grayness settling over the animal hospital in a way that dark clouds could never match. Three more people followed Mrs. Grayson to Old

Doc's that day with pets near to death. Unlike Mrs. Grayson, the owners of these three could not bear to stay till the end.

In their places, Marty stayed with the two old dogs and the cat while Doc sent each in its turn to sleep forever. He couldn't believe that their owners would not remain with their pets till the end, and he told Doc that he thought their leaving was wrong.

"Most of these animals are too sick to know the difference," she told him.

"But *I* know!" Marty frowned. "Are there many days like this—when people bring in piles of animals to be put to sleep?"

"It happens. Vet work goes in cycles like everything else. These pets had good, full lives, Marty, with people who loved them. Two of the dogs we euthanized today were in real pain. I'm relieved I can put them out of their misery humanely. That's part of the job."

Part of the job, Marty thought. Other animals had been put to sleep during the weeks he had been working. He had seen the black plastic garbage bags waiting by the surgery door and known that they were dead animals. But he had never been involved before.

"Why don't you go into surgery, Marty? Both

Charlie and Baby Doc have operations sched-
uled all afternoon and you like surgery. I'll manage fine."

"You're sure?" He was there to work wherever he was needed. He wasn't supposed to care,
at least not much.

"Scoot. Tell Charlie I said you could scrub up
and put on a gown and assist." She waved him
out of the room.

Swaddled in a vast white plastic gown and
wearing sterile gloves, Marty became a sur-
geon's assistant. Again, he was impressed by the
neatness of surgery, by how precise it was, by
the small amount of blood or mess. He learned
the names of instruments and what they were
for. He held retractors to keep the way open to
an animal's interior so that Dr. Switzer or Hank
could work more easily. In the background was
the reassuring beep of steady animal heartbeats
as they were recorded on the electronic monitor.
Dr. Switzer and Hank visited with him and each
other as comfortably as if they'd all been sitting
in the office over Cokes.

At one point Marty asked, "Do you guys know
what makes cats purr? I've always wanted to
know."

Dr. Switzer laughed. "So have we. Nobody

seems to, though—not for sure. Just read an article on that, too. We all agree cats purr, but no one knows exactly why or where it comes from. Hand me some of that gut, Marty. I'm ready to close up."

Silent, Marty watched Dr. Switzer's neat suturing. Being a vet was strange, he thought, and complex. You put an animal to sleep, then gave a new-puppy speech. You operated on others, because if you didn't, *they* might have to be put to sleep. Of course, you couldn't just give new-puppy speeches all the time. Or new-kitten speeches, which were about the same thing. *Kittens.* Marty groaned.

"Got a problem?" Dr. Switzer asked.

11.
Two Down, Four to Go

"Morning, Mrs. Thomas," Marty said as she stepped out onto the porch. He was hurriedly feeding the kittens before school.

"Getting chilly." Mrs. Thomas held her bathrobe closed around her legs. "Marty, there are two families coming this afternoon to pick out kittens. Isn't that wonderful?"

Marty let out a joyful whoop. "I was getting kinda nervous, weren't you? The ad runs today for the second time, so maybe there'll be more calls. Do these people know we've got ordinary kittens, not pedigreed?"

"That's just what they want. Maybe I can talk them into taking two per family. Kittens love being raised with a brother or sister." She picked up one of the kittens and snuggled it.

Marty wondered what he would have done without her. "It sure is good of you to do this. I mean, answering the phone calls, and not telling my mom, and—"

"Hush. It's my Christmas spirit. But, Marty, speaking of Christmas—I'm going to my daughter's house in Indianapolis for the holidays. Your mother's coming over to water my plants and keep an eye on things. We'd better have homes for these kittens by the eighteenth, because then I'll be gone."

"That's only twelve days!" Marty was horrified.

"The ad will have run for the third time, and perhaps by then they'll all be taken. Hadn't you better be on your way to school?" Still holding the kitten, she stood on the porch and waved good-bye as Marty raced down the steps. He hoped his mother wasn't watching from their laundry-room window or she'd wonder why he was at Mrs. Thomas's when he was supposed to be at school. These kittens were a pain.

On the way to school, Marty rehearsed his Careers Week speech. Today was his day to talk, and he was honestly looking forward to it. His dad was right. He'd had real work experience in his own field, and so he ought to be able to give the best talk in class. Well, maybe not the best. *But just about,* he decided confidently.

Marty still felt confident when it was his turn to speak. He stood behind the lectern and didn't rock back and forth the way he had when he'd given his first speech, back in early September. He didn't fiddle with papers either, because all he had to talk from this time was one index card with notes. He remembered to keep eye contact, and to smile as if he were enjoying himself, which he was.

"Veterinary school," Marty explained, "is tough to get into because lots of people want to be vets, and places are limited. Also, the work is hard, so they don't take just anybody. You have to be a good student and want to study a lot, or else there's no point in going to vet school." He paused, then decided to throw in some specific examples, which he knew Mr. Whiting liked to hear.

"Two of the best vet med schools in our area are the University of Pennsylvania and Iowa State University, in Ames, Iowa. Some of you probably go to Doctor Cameron's clinic, where I'm working now, and Doc Cameron went to

Iowa State herself. She finished in five years, but that was a long time ago, and now it takes six or seven years to be a veterinarian." Marty heard two or three kids groan and whisper to each other.

"That's a long time, but think of what they have to know." Marty explained that vets had to learn quite a bit about all kinds of animals. "A person doctor, I mean for humans like us, only has to know *one* body, really, but a vet has to know dozens!" Marty gestured broadly. "And his patients can't talk to say where it hurts, or when it started hurting." He paused to let the weight of his words sink in.

He went on to give some examples of what a vet did in daily work, telling of his trip to the horse barns and the peaceful dairy herd. He told about neutering animals, a frequent event at the vets' office, and when Jimmy Babcock sniggered, Marty shot him a withering look. At that point he felt years older than Jimmy Babcock.

"It's really important to have animals neutered," he said determinedly. "You wouldn't believe how many extra animals we've got in Hampshire. People bring them in all the time and tell us to find homes for them or put them to sleep. *Some people* just leave them, like they were old garbage or something, and *we're* supposed to see that they get good homes."

Marty's class erupted into loud opinions about the cruelty of people who abandoned animals. Mr. Whiting resorted to shouting before the class calmed down. "Martin," Mr. Whiting finally was able to say, "that was excellent. But the class probably has questions now, so let's go into the question period, if you don't mind?"

"How many hours a week does a vet work?" Tim asked. "You work all the time and you're only a helper."

"Raise your hand if you want to speak, Tim," Mr. Whiting said wearily.

"Uh, well." Marty fidgeted slightly. "That's not a good part of this job. My vets—I mean Doc Cameron's group, here in Hampshire—work Monday through Saturday most of the time. Once a month each of them gets a weekend off. But they have evening office hours some days." He stopped and added rapidly in his head. "I guess they work about sixty or sixty-five hours a week." He was surprised himself by the number of hours.

"That stinks," Amy Winters said.

"Sure does," Tim agreed. "Why do they want to do that?" Tim looked directly into Marty's eyes.

Marty gripped both sides of the lectern. He looked down at the neat notes on his index card, but, of course, the answer to Tim's question wasn't there. He remembered asking much the same question of Hank, that Saturday under the oak tree.

At last Marty said the only thing he could say. "I don't know. I guess you have to like the work so much that you don't think of it as work. It's what you want to do, so you do it. Because you care about animals."

The class was silent, respectful of his honesty. It was Jimmy Babcock who broke the silence. "So why do you put animals to sleep then? You send 'em to the pound, too, because our neighbor said so."

"That's dumb!" Amy Winters called out. "They have to put sick animals to sleep or else they'd just hang on in pain, for a long time. Right, Marty?"

Marty nodded. "It's called euthanasia." He could see Old Doc's face the day she'd explained that part of her job. "It isn't easy to do, but

132

Amy's right, sometimes we have to do it." He thought of Mrs. Grayson and Dog.

"And how about the animals you take to the pound?" Jimmy persisted.

"That's not our fault! Those animals are just left there. We can't feed all the stray animals in Hampshire! Or find homes for them either!" He pictured the six orphans on Mrs. Thomas's back porch. *His* orphans.

Mr. Whiting stood up. "Marty, thank you. I think you've been grilled long enough. Thank you for a most informative talk." He clapped, and the class joined in, as Marty gratefully left the lectern and subsided into his seat.

"I didn't get to ask my question," Karen Collier said. "How come they can't cure leukemia in cats? We've had three cats and two of 'em died of cat leukemia!" She looked at Marty as though he should have the answer.

Marty shrugged helplessly. "I don't know. I've only been at Old Doc's a few weeks, but I know feline leukemia's bad. Somewhere, I bet, some vets in labs are working on it. Not all of them work in clinics. I mean, there's got to be research, too, on new medicines."

Mr. Whiting held up both hands. "Thank you

again. Now we must move on to the next talk. Meg, it's your turn."

Marty listened with only half his mind while Meg Turner talked about being a CPA, a certified public accountant. Marty knew he wasn't interested in being an accountant. But was he *only* interested in being a vet? He wished that something would come along and put that pesky voice in his head to sleep—forever.

When Marty arrived for work that afternoon, he was surprised to see Samson leaving. Samson had always been a favorite of Marty's, and he stopped to pet him one last time. "Big day, Samson." Marty looked the owner over, wondering what kind of person would leave her pet with the vet for so long.

"It is a big day," the woman said. "Do you know our cat?"

"I've been feeding and watering him for weeks."

"I see. Well, thank you, then. We've been moving from California and had to rent an apartment that wouldn't allow pets. Now we're in our house and Samson can come home. So you're right. It's a big day for all of us. Good-bye."

"Good-bye, Samson." With a last scratch behind the ears, Marty turned and went into the hospital. Pretty flimsy excuse. *He* wouldn't rent an apartment that didn't allow pets. Pets were family. What was the matter with people anyhow?

In the office, Vicki told Marty that Samson's vet bill had been $147.00 for seven weeks. "Cheaper to leave him behind in California and get a new cat, huh, Marty?"

Marty nudged his glasses into place and stared at Vicki. He couldn't believe she had said that.

"I'm just teasing." Vicki smiled. "Tell Doc there's a lady on line one who says her dog's got a pup stuck that won't deliver. She wants Doc to tell her what to do."

Marty gave Old Doc the message and wandered into Hank's office to see if anything interesting was going on.

Hank greeted him and pointed to a cage on his examining table. "Ever seen ferrets up close? This pair is here for their shots—distemper complex shots, that is."

Marty watched as Hank examined the ferrets and gave their shots. He tried, but he couldn't seem to warm up to them. They looked sneaky. Sort of weasely. Of course, they were weasels, so that made sense.

These ferrets had white fur and very red, beady eyes, and were just over a foot long. One was friendly, but the other did its best to bite Hank. Hank whipped a bandaging strip around its jaws and tied them shut. "Sorry, fella, but I'm attached to the fingers on this hand, and you can't have them."

"He'll bite anything," said the boy standing beside the table. He sounded proud. "Put some ferrets in a cage for a while and take 'em out. Then put a rabbit in that cage. Dumb bunny nearly dies of fright, wonderin' where the ferret is. Ferrets're killers."

Marty examined the boy. He looked about sixteen. Marty thought he must have come from a neighboring town, because he hadn't seen him around Hampshire. Marty didn't like him any better than the ferrets. They even looked like each other.

When the boy and his ferrets had left, Hank admitted to Marty that he wasn't long on ferrets himself. "Give me a nice old tomcat any day, eh, Marty?"

Marty smiled weakly. He could give him a

nice *little* tomcat anytime—plus several other little cats. Briefly, he debated telling Hank about the kittens. But Hank might tell Old Doc. It was bad enough that Jut knew.

That night, when Jut asked how many kittens were left, Marty joyously held up four fingers. "Got rid of two! Two families came to Mrs. Thomas's today to pick out their kittens."

"Four left. Not exactly *shazzam*," Jut observed. "Hey, that reminds me. Look what I got Gus for Christmas. I went shopping after practice." He pulled a shopping bag out of his side of their closet and held up a Superman robot. When he pressed a button, the robot's cape flew out behind him, and the Superman fists made punching motions.

"That's great. Gus'll love it. I don't have anything yet for anybody." Marty remembered that last Christmas he had gone shopping with Tim. They had spent a whole Saturday in the Hampshire shopping mall on the highway outside town. They had had a wonderful time. "I'm going to call Tim," he said.

Late on a Saturday afternoon, only a couple of weeks before Christmas, Marty met Tim at the shopping mall. After two years, the mall was still the talk of the area. It had four restaurants, a video-game parlor, three huge department stores, and umpteen littler stores. "Whole seventh grade's here somewhere," Tim told Marty when they met.

Marty smiled back at Tim and wished he felt like Christmas. Here he was, with money to spend on wonderful presents for the first time in his life, and he couldn't even enjoy it. All because of those kittens.

Marty's ad had run in the *Gazette* for the second time, but there had been no calls. Not even one. What's more, he couldn't talk about it, because only two people knew. In front of Mrs. Thomas and Jut he kept up a brave front, as though the kittens would be gone any day now. But they weren't gone. Instead, the remaining four were eating into Marty's savings and messing up the expensive kitty litter. In just over a week, Mrs. Thomas would be in Indianapolis. *Then what?* Head down, Marty walked through the mall.

"Something wrong? You haven't said a word."

This time Marty didn't even try to smile. "Can you keep a secret?"

"Of course," Tim said. "You oughta know that."

Marty apologized and then told Tim about the kittens. "And I can't take them to the pound, I just can't! After a few days, any animal at the pound is put to sleep."

"Heck, no—not to the pound. I'd take one, but Golda's going to be bred in the spring, and Dad said I could keep a puppy. But probably not if I get a kitten."

"I don't know what else to try. I thought that ad would do it for sure."

Tim was quiet a while. Then he said, "Look, Marty, put it in your back mind for a while and forget it. That's what my mom says. She says not to think about a problem and let your back mind work on it. When you don't even expect it, an answer comes. Know what I mean?"

"She means the subconscious."

"Sure. Way in the back of your mind, not up front. Let's go to the game parlor and buy some presents and eat supper. But don't worry about it, okay? Want to try?"

"Why not?" With effort, Marty smiled. "Let's play Pole Position. I know I can score higher than last time."

Marty and Tim spent an hour and many quarters in the game room. Marty's parents said that electronic games were a waste of time and money, but he had fun anyway and it took his mind off the kittens. He was sure that a few visits to the game parlor wouldn't ruin him forever.

Afterward, the boys shopped for presents. First, Marty bought Jut a dark-green chamois cloth shirt. He was so pleased with it that he bought a bigger one for his dad, in blue, and a smaller one in red for Nick. Until seventh grade, Marty hadn't thought much about clothes, but this year he noticed them. Some clothes were great and others he wouldn't wear no matter what.

For Gus, he bought a set of Lego building blocks. Gus loved to put little pieces of things together, just like Marty had. After three boys, most of the Howards' Lego blocks had been eaten by the vacuum cleaner or were lost in somebody's closet. Now there would be enough for Marty to show Gus how to build a firehouse and truck.

"What're you getting your mom?" Tim asked. "I never know what to get mine."

"Mine's easy. She likes books. I'm going to the bookstore and ask them what's good. I can read the jacket and tell if my mom'll like it or not."

Tim liked that idea, and soon they each had a book for their mothers. "I'm running out of money. I don't make as much on my paper route as you do at the vets'."

"Yeah, I get over thirty dollars a week. I could have spent more, but those kittens cost a fortune. It takes about ten bucks a week for the four that're left, and who knows how long I'll have them?"

"Sorry I said anything. You'll get a good idea, like I said. Let's eat now. I'm starving."

After supper, they went to see *Return of the Jedi*. They had seen it before, but it was worth seeing several times. Marty lost himself in the movie and forgot about the kittens again.

By the time he was home and had hidden his presents in his side of the closet, Marty felt much better. Tim was right. It was stupid to worry about those kittens all the time, because it made him miserable. His mind went around in circles and didn't come up with any good ideas. The thing was to let his subconscious work it out and not sweat it.

Except he had forgotten to give the kittens their supper. He had been too busy with work and shopping. Marty put his jacket back on and called to Jut, who was watching TV in the living room. "Be right back. Got to feed those kittens. When're Mom and Dad coming home?" He couldn't imagine what he would say if his parents caught him sneaking home from Mrs. Thomas's at ten o'clock at night.

"Not till late. They're at a dinner party. Where are you going?"

"I said to feed the kittens! You deaf?"

"You're sure touchy, Marty. Why don't you just take them to the pound and forget it!"

12.
Time Marches On

Marty leaned back in the church pew of Hampshire First Presbyterian and waited for their minister to stop talking. He was a nice man and Marty liked him, but Marty's idea of a good sermon was five minutes and the minister's idea was much longer. Nick and Gus were lucky to be in Sunday School.

Finally, Reverend Parker asked the congregation to bow their heads for the closing prayer. Marty tried to concentrate on what the minister was saying, but concentration was escaping him, as it had a habit of doing lately. Marty thought instead about his problem.

God, Marty begged silently, *please help me*

find homes for the kittens. I don't want anything for myself. But I have to have somewhere for those kittens and I have to have it right away. If You can manage it.

Marty stood up with Jut, his parents, and everyone else to sing the benediction. He had given his problem to God, and he hoped God would get busy and do something. *He* sure didn't know what to do anymore. Mrs. Thomas was leaving in seven days, and the ad for free kittens would run for the last time on Wednesday.

That night Marty finished his weekend's homework in the kitchen, not in his bedroom. Whenever he was alone with Jut, Jut asked if more kittens had been adopted, and Marty wanted to put off that scene as long as possible. He had a science report to write, and that was all he wanted to think about. Mid-quarter report slips would be coming out sometime this week, and he was afraid of what they would show. The Hampshire Junior High teachers were faithful about warning students and parents about slipping grades.

Marty bent his mind to the job at hand and wrote the science report in his neatest handwriting. Nothing, not even the kittens, was going to mess up this assignment.

Monday, Tuesday, and Wednesday raced by, but the telephone did not ring at Mrs. Thomas's house. At least it didn't ring because someone wanted a free kitten, and that was all Marty was interested in hearing.

Wednesday afternoon Marty's feet dragged on the way to work. Snow was falling all around him. Branches had begun to lean down with the weight of it and sidewalks were covered. A heavy snow was unusual in southern Ohio. Everyone he knew was going to Holly Tree Court to build a snow fort. He was going to work.

For the first time, Marty's heart did not fill with pride when he opened the door marked "Hospital Personnel Only." He liked his job and he liked earning money, but today he wanted to build a snow fort. Or he could be home wrapping presents. Or going door-to-door like the good salesman he was, selling free kittens—saying how wonderful it would be to give a child a pet for Christmas.

As he helped John clean cages, Marty wondered why he felt the way he did. Didn't he want to be a vet after all?

"Of course I do," he said out loud.

"How's that?" John stopped wringing out his mop and looked at Marty.

"Nothing—talking to myself."

Just then Old Doc hurried into view. "Come on, boys. We've got the best kind of emergency. A C-section for a nice little schnauzer named Queen Anne. You'll both get to massage a puppy. Forget the cages for now and let's scrub up."

In surgery, Queen Anne lay panting on one of the two larger operating tables. Dr. Switzer was petting the schnauzer and smiling. "Ready?" he asked Old Doc as she, John, and Marty came through the door.

"All set. Troops on hand," Old Doc said as she draped Queen Anne's abdomen with sterile cloths. "This dog was in a car accident when she was younger," she explained to Marty and John. "Now her pelvis is too narrow for a normal birth, so we have to do a cesarean."

Marty watched Queen Anne. "She doesn't seem very asleep. Does she get more anaesthetic?"

"She'll get these," Old Doc said as she began

giving a series of shots down the center of the dog's abdomen. "She's had Inovar, which gives only a light sleep. Don't want those pups to get much anaesthetic. This local anaesthetic will deaden any pain where we'll be operating."

Marty could hardly wait. He watched as she made a long incision down the center of the dog's stomach. In seconds, she pulled the uterus out through the incision, and Marty was astounded at the size of it. It was Y-shaped and over a foot long, and it looked like a very fat sausage.

He remembered another operation, when a cat's uterus had been full of dead kittens. This time would be different.

"How's this compared to the teeny little organ we see when we spay a dog?" Doc asked Marty. She surrounded the bulging uterus with moist, sterile towels and on the end, near the birth canal, made another incision. Then she massaged a puppy through this newly made cut.

"Is he dead?" Marty's eyes fixed on the lifeless little body.

"No, no." She swiftly clamped off the navel cord that had joined the pup to its mother, then wiped the pup's head. "Marty, blow short little breaths toward his mouth to start him breathing and rub him with this towel. Rub him vigorously now. It'll take about a minute and a half."

Marty bent his head to the tiny mouth and blew carefully. His hands rubbed and rubbed, begging the puppy to come to life. *Come on, puppy,* Marty thought. *Hurry up and breathe.*

Several Marty-breaths later, the puppy gasped for air as he moved in Marty's hands. Marty kept on massaging, but let the puppy breathe for himself. He held him against his chest and massaged gently as the puppy breathed and moved his head blindly back and forth. His puppy nose sniffed Marty's shirt.

"He's okay! Look at him, Doc!"

She peered at Marty over the top of her glasses. "Congratulations, you're a mother. Look at his brothers and sisters."

Marty saw that now everyone had a puppy. All, like his, were wrapped in the warm, sterile towels. All of the puppies were breathing—all of them were alive. It was a miracle.

"You hold my baby," Old Doc said, "while I close up. I want to get out of here fast. Better for the mother that way." She handed Marty her swaddled puppy and examined Queen Anne's

rapidly shrinking uterus. "Got to make sure all the afterbirth is out of here," she explained, looking inside the uterus.

Marty cuddled both pups and watched. "Look how fast it goes down!" He was fascinated by the natural wizening of the once-fat organ. "Now it's a hot dog, not a sausage."

Doc laughed. "Nature is something." She replaced the uterus in the dog's abdomen and began suturing the various layers of abdominal muscle back together. When she was finished, she gave the dog a shot of what she called "reverser." Almost immediately, Queen Anne stirred, then sat up and looked around.

"Look! Look at your puppies," Marty said to the schnauzer.

Queen Anne sniffed each puppy and licked it.

"Come on, everybody. Chow time." Doc led the way to a dog cage already prepared with towels and fresh water. She explained to Marty how important it was to put each puppy at its mother's nipple as soon as possible. "They get a substance called colostrum from their first feedings." She hitched her puppy to a nipple as she talked. "It's absolutely essential for them. Colostrum gives immunity from diseases, and after only six or eight hours, the pups can't absorb these antibodies. Got to get this stuff right away."

Marty saw his own puppy and the others greedily sucking in the vital colostrum. "They act like it's a chocolate malt."

"They know what they're doing," Doc said. She looked at Dr. Switzer. "Never gets old, does it, Charlie?"

Marty saw the wide grin on the younger vet's face. He was watching his puppy like a proud new parent, as they all were, Marty realized, looking at John.

"Beats cleaning cages," John said. He petted his puppy.

Marty was the last to leave Queen Anne and her babies. He petted each one in turn. They were special. Lucky puppies. *This* was what being a vet was all about.

He carried the good feeling with him the rest of the afternoon. Before he left, Marty spent time with Gretchen, the last of his long-term boarders. Marty had met Gretchen's owner one afternoon, a friendly older woman who had thanked him for his care of her cat.

"As long as my son and his children are with

me, Gretchen has to stay here," she had told him. "The children are too young and too naughty. They gave Gretchen a shower one day—locked her in the car—put her in the oven. I can't stand it. I was afraid Gretchen would run away. She's better off here, and I'll just come to visit her. As soon as my son gets a job, they'll move, and I'll come for Gretchen."

On his way home, Marty stopped by Mrs. Thomas's to feed the kittens and ask if anyone had called.

Mrs. Thomas shook her head. "I'm sorry, Marty. I wish I didn't have to leave on Sunday, but I've had my plane ticket for weeks. Maybe people will call this evening after they've had a chance to read the *Gazette*."

Maybe, Marty thought, as he kicked up clouds of snow in his backyard. Now only three days were left before Mrs. Thomas went to Indianapolis. Who would have thought he'd have so much trouble giving away something as wonderful as kittens?

13.
Get Your Free Kittens Here!

Mr. Howard stopped poking at his fireplace logs and turned to Marty. "What do you think of your mid-quarter slips? Are those grades what you expected?"

"What I expected. Not what I hoped to get." Marty figured that honesty was the only way. He hated discussions with his parents about grades. Didn't they know he cared more than they did?

Marty's mother put the slips into the pocket in Marty's notebook. "I signed them so you can give them back to your homeroom teacher on Monday. Your grades aren't down much, Marty, but it's a concern. We have to think that your job is taking way too much time."

"When report cards come, the end of January, they'll be about normal. Don't worry, okay? They're my grades."

"True," Mr. Howard agreed, "but we wouldn't be very good parents if we weren't interested, now, would we?"

Marty nodded. He had heard those words before. He wondered if all parents said exactly the same things. Would he talk to his kids this way when he was a father?

"You're down a grade in science, English, and math, Marty. Do you know what to do to bring those grades up to where they were last marking period?" Mrs. Howard wasn't going to give up easily.

Quitting my job would do it, Marty admitted to himself. He had not had enough time for homework in many weeks. But did he want to quit his job? Marty looked down at his sneakers. He didn't want to quit, exactly, but he was beginning to wish there were less job somehow. Fewer hours. He had seen the big snow fort on Holly Tree Court. And Tim and Rusty and other friends were tobogganing on the hills in Hampshire Park.

"Let me work on it, Mom. I can work it out if I just have some time." Marty wanted the conversation to end.

Mr. Howard put his hand on Marty's shoulder. "We'll leave it that way. I don't want you to think we're being negative or critical, Marty, but we are concerned."

Marty nodded. "Okay. Okay," and left the living room. Even if Jut asked him about the kittens, he wanted to be in his room right now.

"Hey," Jut said in greeting as Marty opened their door and walked in. "You survived."

"Just barely." Marty's voice was doleful.

"It's because you're the big brain of the family. They think you ought to get all A's."

Marty sighed. "I've got nothing but problems, not brains. I sure could have lived without those mid-quarter slips."

"Still got four kittens? When does Mrs. Thomas leave?"

"She leaves Sunday, day after tomorrow, and yes, there are still four kittens."

Jut didn't say anything for a minute. He piled his books into a neat stack. "Look, Marty, I'm sorry. But I don't know what to do. If you think of how I can help, I'll help, okay?"

"It has to be done tomorrow, whatever it is. After Mrs. Thomas leaves, Mom's in charge of her house. You know how she is. She'll whip right over there and check everything out. I just can't leave those kittens on the porch."

"I know." Jut took off his shoes and scratched one foot with the other. "How about taking them downtown tomorrow? It's Saturday, and everybody'll be in town shopping. We can stand by Stone's department store or someplace, right by the door, and see if people won't take one. What about that?"

Marty lifted his chin off his chest. It wasn't the best idea he'd ever heard, but it wasn't the worst either. And Jut was willing to help. "Geez, Jut, thanks. I was getting worried, and—"

"You've been worried about *something* ever since you took that job," interrupted Jut. He looked sharply at Marty. "And don't get all mad. You know I'm right. Let's just go to bed and forget it. Tomorrow we'll give them away downtown and that'll be that."

Marty didn't argue and he didn't get mad, because he knew Jut was right. He pushed his books to the back of the desk and got ready for bed. He was tired. He wanted to sleep and forget about animals that were orphans.

When Marty woke up on Saturday morning, Jut was already pulling on a sweatshirt. "Come on, Marty. Let's get going. Maybe we'll be all out of kittens by noon and you can go to work."

"That'd be wonderful." Marty yawned and tried to feel optimistic, like Jut. "I've got to call Doc. Yesterday, when I left, I said I might have family business today."

After Marty called Old Doc, he and Jut ate cereal and peanut butter toast. "I'm going to work later," Marty told his mother, "so Jut and I are going downtown, okay?"

"That's fine, but don't forget to round up the trash later this afternoon, boys." She tied Gus's scarf around his neck. "Can you take Gus, by any chance?"

"No way," Jut answered. "He can go sledding with me later. Sorry, Mom."

Marty and Jut left quickly, while their mother explained to Gus that it was hard to be the littlest.

The boys put out food for the four kittens and talked with Mrs. Thomas while the cats ate. Then they put the four in their box and walked downtown through the snow.

Hampshire was decked out for the holidays. Shimmery silver garlands wound from one light pole to the next. Storefronts beckoned with frosty decorations or traditional window displays. On the major street corners, glittering red bells dangled from the silver garlands stretched across the intersections. A Salvation Army band played "O Come, All Ye Faithful" while a red-faced man in a uniform rang a bell continuously. As long as Marty could remember, Christmas had looked and sounded just like this.

"Let's try Stone's first," Jut suggested. "They do lots of business, so we'll see more people there."

Marty and Jut stood by the main doorway to Stone's department store, right in front of the window depicting the manger scene. The manger scene had been in this window every Christmas. Marty noticed that Mary's blue gown was peeling and Joseph's nose was chipped. The baby Jesus, in his manger, looked in better shape. Around the manger were sheep, cows, and a donkey. Hay and straw covered the floor of the window, just in case anyone doubted that this was really a stable.

"Looks just the same," Marty said contentedly. He would not have liked it to be different.

"Here comes a couple," Jut whispered. "They look like parents. Offer 'em a nice kitty."

Marty plunged his hand into the box and held up a gray-and-white kitten. "Pardon me, but wouldn't you like to give somebody a pet for Christmas? This kitten needs a good home."

The couple looked at each other, shook their heads, and went on into Stone's. Marty put the kitten back into the box.

"Hi, there," he said to the next likely-looking couple. "Free kittens for Christmas presents?" He dangled a tiger kitten under their noses.

This couple said, almost in one voice, "Thanks. We've got some of our own at home."

Next, Marty tried a few older women who looked lonely. They didn't want a kitten either. Neither did a man who looked like a grandpa, or the high school principal. The principal petted the kittens, visited with Jut about the school basketball season, then went about his shopping.

After an hour, Marty was discouraged. He had said every good thing he could think of and nothing had worked. Just like the ad in the paper hadn't worked. All the kids who came by wanted to see what was in the box and hold a kitten. All the adults wanted to get out of sight as quickly as possible.

"Let's try the kids' clothing store," Jut suggested.

Parents, grandparents, aunts, and uncles came and went through the Tiny Togs doors, but none of them wanted kittens. One man laughed at Marty and said, "You've got to be kidding!" Marty wanted to punch him in the nose.

By noon, Marty and Jut were cold clear through. They closed the cardboard lid on the kitten box and carried it into the dime store where they could eat lunch and warm up.

"I thought they'd be gone by now," Jut said through a mouthful of hot dog. "I don't believe this is happening."

"I believe it." Marty swirled cocoa around in his mug. "I shouldn't have taken them from the vets'. But I thought it'd be easy. The puppies were easy."

After lunch, Marty, Jut, and the kittens stood in front of the hardware store, the florist's, and the Grove Street Market. The town was full of people who knew how to say no to a free kitten.

No matter how well Marty phrased his speech, the answer was always no.

At two o'clock, Jut said, "Marty, we've got to try something else. Let's walk back toward Stone's and see what we can think up."

Marty closed the flaps on the kitten box and followed silently. His feet were numb with cold and so were his hands. He couldn't feel sorry for the kittens any longer, but he felt very sorry for himself. Why did this have to be so hard?

Back at Stone's, they stood again in front of the window with the manger scene. Marty looked at the window, not out at the people. He had given up on the people. *You were supposed to help*, he thought, staring accusingly at Jesus in the manger.

The baby Jesus, made of wood and paint, stared blankly back at Marty. Marty looked away from him and inspected the cows, which were made all wrong. Their tails were too short and their heads too long. Somebody hadn't known much about real live cows. The sheep were better, but not woolly enough. It was too fake, all of a sudden, to suit Marty. In a real barn there was movement, there was life. It made all the difference.

"Oh boy!" Marty stared harder into the manger scene. Yes, it would be perfect. Warm and safe. "Hey, Jut, look at this window."

Jut turned, blowing on his hands to warm them.

"What's missing in this window? What would make people stop and look, and then go inside the store that was *smart* enough to have such a terrific window?"

Jut looked at Marty as if he were crazy. "How do I know? Just tell me. I'm too cold to guess."

"Something live!" Marty announced triumphantly. "It would draw people to the window and then into the store."

Jut frowned in concentration, then began to smile. "You mean the kittens, right?"

"That's it! See, we'll put a sign in the window saying 'FREE KITTENS' in big letters. Anybody shopping in town will have a whole week to pick a kitten out for a Christmas present. It's perfect!"

Marty bent down, grabbed up the box of kittens, and headed for the door into Stone's.

Behind him, Jut said, "I don't know, Marty. You'll have to convince the store manager they won't be any trouble."

"Just watch me," Marty said, remembering how he had convinced Dr. Dinsmore that the orphanage needed two puppies.

After a short wait in an outer office, Marty, Jut, and the kittens were allowed to talk to the manager.

"What can I do for you boys?" The manager, a Mr. Stone, Jr., looked friendly.

"I have a great way to bring people into the store," Marty began, knowing he would want to do just that if he were a store manager.

Marty continued, explaining how the kittens would be "eye-catching" in the window, how everyone would stop to see them play in the straw, climb on the back of the gray wooden donkey, mew at the window. He fished the cutest kitten out of the box and held him up. "Who wouldn't love watching this kitten chase his tail? It'd turn your window into a real live barn. It'd be the *only* window in town!"

Mr. Stone reacted much the way Dr. Dinsmore had. He was overwhelmed. At last he said, "But why do you want to do this?"

"Because these kittens have to find homes or they're going to the pound. *At Christmastime*." He held the kitten to his chest protectively.

"I see. Well, you've got a very sound idea, and I have no objections. But you will have to set it up and maintain the window yourself. My help is frantic during the holidays. Is that okay with you?"

It was more than okay. "No problem," Marty assured Mr. Stone, Jr. "I'll feed them on my lunch hour, before noon, and at night before the store closes. I'll put up the sign, too. Can the clerks near the window give away a kitten if somebody wants one?"

"I can arrange that. We'll go down there now—that's the shoe and sock department—and tell those clerks what's going on. I'll show you how to get into the window." He stood up behind his desk. "And see if you can't hide their litter pan, know what I mean?" He smiled at Marty and Jut. Jut nodded, still silent with admiration for Marty.

In no time at all, the kittens were in the window, delighted to be out of their box, delighting the people who gathered around the window.

Marty and Jut collected all the kittens' food, bowls, and litter from Mrs. Thomas's back porch. Marty made a sign that said, "FREE CHRISTMAS KITTENS. Ask inside." Back at the window, he posted the sign at eye level, hid the litter pan behind Jesus and the manger, and put out fresh food and water.

Mr. Stone, Jr., came to see how Marty's idea was working out. From the inside of the store, he and the boys peered into the window. On the outside, people were standing three deep to get a look at the kittens. One kitten hopped up to the manger and sat down on baby Jesus's stomach to wash his face. The crowd responded with laughter.

"Looks pretty good," Mr. Stone, Jr., said to Marty.

"It's very psychological," Marty murmured to the manager. "Know what I mean?"

"I certainly do," replied Mr. Stone, Jr. "Now if you want to come in on Sunday, you'll have to do it in the morning, around nine, with the maintenance crew. Will that be all right?"

"Sure. I'll put out enough food for the day. And thanks a lot, I really mean it." Marty held out his hand.

Outside, Marty and Jut joined the people jammed in front of Stone's unique Christmas window. Marty watched the kittens and thought he had never been so glad to get rid of anything in his life. He gazed once more at the baby Jesus. "Sorry," he whispered. "I didn't mean it."

14.
Six Shopping Days Left

Early on Sunday, Marty headed downtown to feed the kittens in Stone's window display. He told his mother he was going to round up a group to go sledding in the afternoon, but he knew she suspected something. She had said things like, "Why don't you call them on the phone?" and "You can talk to them after church." He had fended off all objections and bolted out the door before she said anything final.

You guys are a royal pain, he thought as he cleaned the kitty litter and put out fresh water and food. The kittens tried to climb his leg and purred as they inspected his boots.

After church and lunch, all the Howard boys

went to Hampshire Park to toboggan or sled. "Be sure to watch out for Gus," Mrs. Howard reminded them. "Dad will come around three to take him home. He'll have had enough by then."

"No I won't," Gus told his mother.

"Yes you will," Marty said, pulling Gus out the door. The older boys stayed on the hills until nearly dark. They made so many runs down the hills that Marty's legs were rubbery as they walked home.

Sunday night Marty did his homework in peace. He wrote another book report with almost no misery. The last one had earned him an A minus, which he needed, and he was praying to repeat that reward.

Monday in school was just as peaceful as Sunday night had been. Marty concentrated almost all day, fed the kittens at lunch, had a great snowball fight after lunch, and never once worried about orphans. He had turned the kittens over to the baby Jesus and Stone's department store.

Marty aimed a few snowballs at light posts on the way to work that afternoon. He didn't want to work again, and that bothered him. What if there were more puppies or kittens without homes waiting for him at the hospital? He knew now that it was always possible. When John had said, "There'll be more," he had been right.

Somehow, Marty's job at the vet hospital had become linked with orphan animals. He knew it was his own fault, if it were a fault, but he didn't know what to do about it. And his job was linked to falling grades in school. He knew what to do about that. Quit the job.

Marty stewed. He realized he was worrying. Again. *Rats,* he thought, watching his snowball land splat, dead center on a light pole.

Marty shut the hospital door behind him and listened to the familiar yips and barks that made a pattern of sound he still loved. A waiting-room cat hissed at some imagined threat, and a dog whined low in answer. A woman's voice said, "Muffy always tells us when she's got a fur ball." The mat under Marty's feet smelled faintly of manure, and over it all hovered the odor of disinfectant.

How can I give up this job?

Old Doc's voice broke in. "Marty, go get Tootie and Sniffles Melbourne. I'll meet you all in my room after I handle a phone call." She whisked off toward the telephone.

"TOOTIE AND SNIFFLES MELBOURNE?" Marty boomed in the entryway to the waiting room. *Someday,* he imagined, *a patient will say, "Right here, Dr. Howard."*

A young woman rose from the bench in answer to Marty's call. Attached to one hand was a leash, and at the end of it was a handsome Great Dane. Marty thought he looked like a small horse. The hand that held the leash pushed a baby stroller, and in the stroller was a boy about two years old. The woman picked up a cat carrier and came toward Marty. "This is all of us for today," she said brightly.

"You mean there are more?" he asked. Mrs. Melbourne nodded and led the way down the hall.

"Who's Tootie and who's Sniffles?" Marty asked Mrs. Melbourne when they got inside Doc's examining room. He shut the door just in case the Great Dane bolted.

"Tootie's the dog. Let's get him up on the table so we're ready for Dr. Cameron." She pushed the stroller into a corner.

Marty lowered the examining table. He was glad Mrs. Melbourne was familiar with the routine, but he couldn't imagine how he was going to coax Tootie up onto the table if he didn't want to go.

Table down on floor level, Marty leaned over and looked into Tootie's tan-colored face. "Here you go," he said, patting the table. Mrs. Melbourne pulled on the leash and Tootie obligingly hauled himself up onto the table. He rode upward in dignified silence.

"Hey, he's easier than the little dogs."

"Oh, Danes are wonderful pets," Mrs. Melbourne said. "They're gentle and strong and lovable, everything you want a dog to—No, no, Tommy, you can't get out of your stroller." She bent down and stuffed Tommy back into his seat.

Old Doc came in, pushing her stethoscope down into her pocket. "And how are the Melbournes today? Is this Rootie or Tootie?"

"We left Rootie at home. She doesn't have this itch like Tootie does, and I hope it's not catching."

Doc peered at the Melbournes' pet charts. Marty wondered why they had so many charts and who Rootie was. "Rootie?" he asked.

"Rootie's Tootie's mate," Mrs. Melbourne explained. "They're quite a pair. Last year Rootie had ten puppies. That's when Tommy was only

171

a year old. I won't forget that experience in a hurry." She laughed and shook her head. "Of course, some of the pups are gone now."

Marty's eyes widened. *Several Great Danes— plus a cat—in one family.* And his mother thought *they* had a lot of pets.

Old Doc examined Tootie, prescribed a salve for the itchy place, and rubbed some in. "Probably just an allergy. Or a place he's worrying, time after time. We call those hot spots," she said. "And how about Sniffles?"

"She just needs her cat shot," Mrs. Melbourne replied. "But I may be back with Bats later on this week. He seems listless to me, awfully droopy."

"*Bats?*" Marty asked.

"He's our other cat. Sniffles' mate." Mrs. Melbourne put Sniffles on the table once Tootie was on the floor.

Marty was keeping count of Melbourne animals. "Did Sniffles have kittens?"

"Yes, she has a litter about once a year. Darling things, too, but we may have her spayed one of these days. I get so tired of lugging home the cat and dog food, you know."

Stunned, Marty nodded.

"Did Charlie get out this weekend to see Oompa and Whimsy?" Old Doc asked. She was examining the pet charts.

"Yes, he was by late Saturday afternoon. Oompa just has a virus, like a cold, and he gave Whimsy a shot for that stiffness in her left foreleg. Whimsy seems better already. I rode her next day, yesterday that was, and she's much less stiff. I didn't ride for long, of course. Charlie's just wonderful with animals, isn't he?"

"Oompa and Whimsy?" Marty couldn't help asking.

"Oompa's our donkey and Whimsy's my mare. The mare's getting old, though, and we may have to get another. If I can't ride every day, I get grumpy. Don't I, Tommy?" She petted Tommy's head just as if he were a dog.

Marty's mental calculator was whirring. "Do you live on a farm?"

"Yes, on the road to Greenville. You know," she said, to Old Doc, "Oompa still misses Sherlock. They were great friends, and it was such fun to see them together."

Before Marty could ask, Old Doc said, "Sherlock was their bloodhound. We lost him to gastric torsion. Those deep-chested dogs are subject

173

to bloat, and sometimes we can't do a thing about it. Damned shame." She put Sniffles back in her cat cage. "Anything else today?"

"That's it." Mrs. Melbourne put Tootie's leash on her wrist, turned Tommy's stroller, and picked up the cat cage.

Marty went ahead of her to open the door. He was dying to ask if they had any more animals. Old Doc came up behind him as he shut the door. "Those folks keep me in business," she said, smiling. "Never saw people so crazy about animals. Her husband's the same way."

"Is she for real?"

"Certainly. We've a few other families like that. Truth, Marty, is a whole lot stranger than fiction." She turned. "Come on. You Clorox my table and I'll get our next patient."

Marty lost himself in the afternoon routine of the vet hospital. He Cloroxed the table, got medicines for Doc from the dispensary, cleaned cages with John. He didn't ask if the two puppies in the end cage belonged to someone or not because he was afraid to find out.

On the way home, he saw that somebody had added a wing to the snow fort on Holly Tree Court. It was beginning to look like a little castle, he thought wistfully. He grabbed up some snow and made a perfectly round ball, which he turned round and round in his mittened hands. He guessed he was going to have to make some decision about his job after all. This way was too hard.

Marty kicked his boots off in the garage and went inside to put his mittens in front of a hot air register. For once, he'd finished all of his homework in school.

"That you, Marty?" his mother called from the kitchen.

"Yup. Is supper ready?"

"Yes, but first you should call Mr. Stone." Mrs. Howard met him at the kitchen doorway. "Of Stone's department store. Why is he calling you?"

15.
A Decision

Marty froze in the kitchen doorway. He had forgotten to feed the kittens on his way home from work. And, worse than that, he had forgotten to tell Mr. Stone not to call him at home.

Marty ran a hand through his hair. "Mom, I'll tell you in just a minute. First, let me call Mr. Stone." He brushed past her and ran upstairs to use the phone in private. He needed to think about what he was going to say to his mother.

"Mr. Stone? This is Marty Howard. I forgot all about feeding the kittens tonight. But I think they'll be okay till morning."

"They'll be fine, especially since there are only two left."

Marty leaned against the headboard of his parents' bed and gave silent thanks. "Somebody took *two*?"

"Yes. First thing this morning. A woman said she was going to give them to her children for Christmas, and weren't we a wonderful store to think of it." His voice was warm. "Marty, I'm sure they'll be gone in no time. Do you think you could get me some more for next Christmas? We've had people at our window all day."

"Sure I can get some for next year!" Marty wondered just how many kittens he could place if he had a whole holiday season to work with.

"Good night, then. See you in the morning." Mr. Stone, Jr., hung up the telephone.

Now there were only two kittens to place. If no one wanted them, Marty would have to find them homes. But at least he was down to two.

Marty got to his feet inch by inch. He would have to tell his mother something. He went down the hall, hoping that Jut was in their room. It would be nice to have Jut around when he explained about the kittens, because that's what he was going to do—explain, and get it over with.

Jut was lying on his bunk, listening to the radio and staring at the underside of Marty's bunk.

"You want to come downstairs? I have to tell Mom about the kittens. Mr. Stone called and she took the message."

"He told her?" Jut slid off the bed and stood up.

"Just said to call him. She wants to know why."

Jut nodded. "I missed all my free throws today. Played our worst game all season. If we can have a big fat argument, maybe I can forget about it." He shrugged his shoulders and smiled at Marty.

"We aren't going to have any argument," Marty said determinedly as he went down the hall. "I handled it, and there's no problem."

"That's true, you know that?" Jut followed him down the steps and into the kitchen. "I thought you did great."

Marty found his mother reading a book at the kitchen table. She looked up as he and Jut came into the room. "You called Mr. Stone?"

"Yes. He's had some kittens in his store window, in the manger scene. I gave him the kittens to see if people wouldn't take them home for presents. They're free."

"From Doc Cameron's?"

"Yes. Just like the puppies I gave away."

"And Gooney Pig?" She smiled encouragingly.

"It's a real problem vets have, Mom. A terrible problem. People leave animals there all the time. Or bring healthy ones in to be put to sleep. These kittens were in the waiting room one night, shut up in a box."

Mrs. Howard closed her book. "That certainly is a problem. What does Doc Cameron say about it?" She bent down and picked up Eleanore, who had been curled up on a rag rug by her feet. Absently, she petted the cat while she waited for Marty's answer.

Marty didn't think that Doc had ever discussed stray animals with him. "Well, she keeps them when she can. Feeds them. Puts signs in the waiting room. After a while, they get sent to the pound."

"But you can't do that, is that it?"

Marty nodded.

"I feel the same way you do, Marty. It's awful." Her hands rested lightly on Eleanore's furry length. "But as long as you work there, that will be part of the job."

Marty shifted his feet. "The rest of the job's great. I don't even mind cleaning cages anymore. It's just all those . . . those *extra* animals!"

Mrs. Howard stood up and put Eleanor down on her chair. "That's what they are, extra. But you need to decide what's good for *you* and what isn't. Taking on the problems of that vet hospital hasn't been easy."

"But I'm good at it! Old Doc said so."

"I'm sure you are or you wouldn't be there. That's not the point. Is *it* good for *you*?"

Marty thought that truth was sometimes awful. He didn't want to answer his mother because her question was too close to what he'd been asking himself.

Behind him, Jut spoke. "Maybe he could sort of compromise. Just work every other day or something?"

Marty considered Jut's idea. The job he had now was every day except Sunday. Maybe, if he talked to Old Doc about it, she would have an answer. "I'll talk to Doc. Let me work on it, okay?" He turned to Jut. "Thanks." He would have said more, but he couldn't think how to say it.

"Glad to be of service." Jut grinned. "What's for supper?"

On Tuesday, before lunch, Marty left school and jogged downtown to feed the kittens. Only one kitten greeted Marty in the window. Its littermate, a gray-and-white female, had gone to her new home just before Marty arrived. "Did the people say where they lived?" Marty asked the clerk who had given away the cat.

"Just north of here, on a farm. She'll be a barn cat, in charge of mouse extermination." The clerk, a young man, smiled proudly at Marty. "Sure is fun to give them away."

Marty knew the feeling.

Just then, an elderly couple stopped at the sock counter where Marty and the clerk were talking. "You say that cat in the window is free?" asked the man.

"Yessir!" Marty didn't even give the clerk a chance.

"We'll take it," the woman said to Marty. "We lost our old tomcat back in the fall and we miss him. Our house's full of cracks and mice come in, especially in the cold weather. He a good mouser?"

"The best! He's the nicest Christmas present you could give yourselves. I'll get him right now." Marty hopped up into the window display, found the last kitten asleep in the manger with baby Jesus, and gently lifted him up. "You're going home," he told the kitten. He smiled down at the baby in the manger.

That evening, after work, Marty didn't have to go anywhere to feed orphan animals. For now, he didn't have a single homeless thing to worry over. *And I don't want any,* he said to himself. Maybe he should see if Doc was in her office before he left.

"You busy?" he asked, seeing her bent over papers on her desk. He almost hoped she was too busy to talk. He wanted an answer—and he didn't. What a dumb way to feel.

"Come in. Just going over some records. What's on your mind?" She took off her glasses and rubbed her eyes.

He didn't know where to begin. He sat down on Doc's two-seater sofa and looked at his knees.

"Did an animal die that I don't know about?"

Marty looked up. "No. Not that I know of."

"Are you having trouble saying something?" She smiled.

"I don't know how to say it."

"Let me help you. Does it have something to do with the job?"

"Well . . . ," Marty answered.

"Are you thinking that the bad parts out-weigh the good parts? For you, anyway?"

"Kinda. But not all the time." He remem-bered the schnauzer puppy he had brought to life. *No. Not all the time.* "But people, other people, don't care much about animals."

"And you do. All the time, not just sometimes? And all of the animals?"

"I don't like horses much. And I hate ferrets. That's not it, or anyway, that's not important."

"You're right. That's not important. Baby Doc dislikes horses . . . and I'm not much on ferrets myself. But I've had a long time to sort this all out, and you haven't. You know, I wasn't always a vet."

"What were you first?"

"A lab technician. Hated it. So, at twenty-five, I put myself into vet school and starved for five years. Of course, now it's nearer seven, even eight years for some. But anyway, that's how old I was when I knew what I wanted to do with myself."

"I thought I knew."

"I know that. That's why I let you work here— to help you find out. But why pick a career now?" She came over to sit beside him on the sofa.

"I don't know. I just thought I had." Marty sighed.

Doc shook her head. "You'll have dozens of careers to pick from, Marty. For one, you can sell anything. What if you became a buyer and seller of livestock? Or a vet med teacher or animal technician? All kinds of jobs can mix animals into a career without being a vet."

Marty hadn't thought much about other animal jobs. "How's come you think I can sell?"

Doc leaned back against the sofa. "One. Sold guinea pig to your mother. Two. Sold three puppies—one to Jason Markham, who brought his pup in last Saturday for puppy shots. Other two puppies now live at the orphanage and are coming in for shots the end of the week. Three. Six kittens ballyhooed around town, now probably in homes unknown. But I'll see them in the office sooner or later." She grinned broadly.

"Who told you?"

"I have my sources. I get around, you know. And John can't keep a secret."

So now it was all out in the open. "What should I do? Should I quit? I'm no good this way."

"Wrong. You're one of the finest employees anyone could have. No bull, Marty. But you've gone at this pretty hot and heavy. How about coming in just on Saturdays? Give yourself a little distance from it—time to decide how you feel about veterinary medicine."

There it was, the compromise Jut had suggested. Marty sat up straight. "I can decide *not* to decide!" For the first time during their talk, he smiled.

"You betcha. And I never send animals to the pound on Saturdays." She gave him a calculating look.

"And," she continued, "I can call you in for every cesarean, if you want. You see, I think the wonderful side is far more important than the bad side to this career. I see what we can do for animals that wasn't possible even five years ago. That's why I'll never quit." She got up from the couch.

"Can't you see me now? An old, stooped lady

with a cane and a hearing aid?" She bent over and cupped a hand to her ear. "You say your pigs've got scours?" Her voice was squeaky old. "Why'd you call me out here if you know what your pigs've got?"

Marty laughed. And suddenly wanted to find her an extra-special Christmas present. He would shop for it tomorrow afternoon, after school. On Saturday, Christmas Eve day, he would come here to work.

Then he would wait and see—and someday decide.

The End